A Series of Failed Suicidal Careers
Book 1: Jeanna Rose

By Roslyn J. Daniel

ROSLYN DANIEL

DEDICATION

There are millions of people struggling
to LIVE out the 86,400 seconds of each DAY
This Book is for THEM.

This book is also dedicated to
my daughter Rachel Elisabeth
My "one and only" and
Most Favored of All, Loved by God

ROSLYN DANIEL

The spiritual life does not come cheap. It is not a stroll down a Mary Poppins path with a candy-store God who gives sweets and miracles. It is a walk into the dark with the God who is the light that leads us through darkness.

Darkness, I have discovered, is the way we come to see.

It creates the depressions that, once faced, teach us to trust. It gives us the sensitivity it takes to understand the depth of the pain in others.

It seeds in us the humility it takes to learn to live gently with the rest of the universe. It opens us to new possibilities within ourselves.

Darkness is a very spiritual thing.

—from <u>Called to Question</u>: A Spiritual Memoir by Joan Chittister

ROSLYN DANIEL

ACKNOWLEDGMENTS

This fictional novel would not be possible were it not for the brave people who shared their journeys, losses, tragedies, traumas, and yes, <u>FAILED SUICIDE</u> attempts with a listener unversed in the language of their suffering. The stories and characters are not real, but the illustrations used to describe the psycho-social context of suicide are true. Special thanks to the resources I tapped into to fill in the pieces of this story: **The American Psychological Association DSM-IV, New Jersey Traumatic Loss Coalition,** The National Alliance for Mental Illness (**NAMI), The American Society for Suicide Prevention, The National Institute for Mental Health** (NIMH), **The Substance Abuse and Mental Health Services Administration,** (SAMHSA), and a host of websites like WebMD.com, Suicide.org, and others, whose fundamental information and materials were used for illustrative purposes solely.

A final acknowledgment goes to the work of Dr. Roy Baumeister at Florida State University, whose dedicated suicidality research been vital in suicide prevention.

Why People Want to Die

"Out of frustrations, out of desperation, out of disappointments, out of mediocrity. out of idleness, out of limited insight, out of difficulties, out of insatiability, out of poverty, out of pain and the vicissitudes of life, so many people shall come to a conclusion that nothing is worth living for; not even what is solemn and sacred but, some shall always turn the woes of life into great land marks and indelible footprints worth emulating"

— Ernest Agyemang Yeboa

1- "STILL HERE?"

Lethargic and dazed, Jeanna Rose Audrey Thornton awakened from her coma. She laid there, bewildered that she remained alive. Her medical chart read like it the description of any single, slightly overweight, 43- year old African American female: "5'8", 213lbs, unmarried. No children. Occupation: Lawyer. Unknown drug or alcohol history. Diagnosed with Dysthymia in 1998. Suicide attempt indicated". Of course, like all institutions focused on pathology and statistics, the record did not mention that this was Jeanna's first act of self-immolation, planned after months of dejected ideations, weeks of preparation. No one knew how the days of anticipation filled Jeanna with a strangely exhilarating hope in dying. Of course, there was no prescription for how to deal with the shock of actually surviving a suicide attempt; Jeanna would have to solve that weighty challenge on her own.

As slow realization, and, brutally painful symptoms emerged, Jeanna became terrified; mental fogginess shrouded her concentration, which, at first, she perceived as heaven, and then, hell. "Oh my God, This can't be death, or is it?" Wonderment and dismay provoked her demand, "God, how in hell am I STILL HERE?" Jeanna felt like s@#&, as some apparently foreign mass thrashed around in her head like a wild bull, kicking, stamping and boring into her skull angrily. Whose throbbing, swollen tongue filled her mouth? And why, **how**, was she STILL ALIVE?

Rosedale Medical Center doctors and her church's intercessors waged warfare to revive her collapsing central nervous system, failing kidneys and liver, until finally, with all therapeutic options exhausted, the physicians resorted to the controversial antidote, Flumazenil. After several infusions, the curative worked to flush out most of the twenty-two benzodiazepine capsules Jeanna swallowed.

While unconscious, Jeanna seemed paralyzed, with the exception of involuntary spasms in her legs. The ventilator was removed three days ago after her vitals were stabilized, but she remained as insentient as a rock, until something, she believed it was God, aroused her this morning. Dora Lynn Thornton-White, whom Jeanna lovingly referred as Grandma Dora, slumbered in the recliner chair beside the hospital bed and nightstand, unaware that her only grandchild was now fully revived; Jeanna needed it to remain that way. The disgrace she was certain her actions heaped upon Grandma Dora and the Thornton clan, all prominent leaders in Rosedale, Georgia since Reconstruction, made her feel too heart-sick and ill-prepared for the judgments sure to follow, so she feigned unconsciousness.

Sure, her deception was cowardly, she thought, but fear was a powerful incentive, so she remained silent as drunkenness caused her to slip in and out of consciousness. Nausea, a side-effect of the medications, pitilessly attacked her system with a vengeance, which pissed Jeanna off. Despite the distress, Jeanna was conscious enough to know she needed more than bravery to answer the inevitable whys she would encounter. She suspected people would even have the nerve to just come right out, just like the church mother's did and ask things like, "Girl, what ails you? What's wrong with you trying to kill yourself? Don't you know that ain't nothing but the devil?" There was no greater horror, it seemed, than to have failed to complete a carefully devised suicide, especially after having heaped venom on one's enemies. Jeanna's botched attempt felt like she had given finger to the driver who cut her off in the road then drove off heading into death's sunset, before being stopped (figuratively) at the red light, right next to her victim. What would she do? In Jeanna's mind, she'd already given the entire world and its ilk her middle one, and now, unless she died soon (considering the agony she suffered), consequences were unavoidable.

Mockery, pity, disparagement, all of the above were waiting at the hospital exit Jeanna surmised as she shivered in her hospital gown. An unknown future loomed before Jeanna and in her state, it was too much to consider. Courage apparently flushed out with the poisons as Jeanna saw nothing but vague, disconsolate sufferings on the horizon. Fear and agonizing discomfort snaked through her abdomen, along with a fever that parched her throat. While the punishing sickness lingered around like a bad date, her grandmother, Dora Thornton-White remained comfortably at rest; she would be the hardest to face.

How does a suicidal person explain their actions to the most cherished surrogate mother on earth? Most pressing was how Jeanna would move forward with the life she still possessed, having discarded the notion months ago? Questions about how she would function beyond the catastrophe of her attempt, and many other confounding puzzles, lay before Jeanna in thousands of jumbled pieces.

The predicament agitated her still-fuzzy conscience. She considered, between earth-shattering thralls of stomach pain, how her grandmother must have felt while maintaining her constant bedside vigil and the anxiety she bore while praying for her only grandchild to awaken. "Grandma Dora, I'm so sorry I've put you through even more sadness!" Jeanna imagined there must have been a great hullabaloo of confusion, all managed by her pintosized heroine. She was struck with something greater than shame - regret.

Jeanna knew that besides kin and nosey folks from Rosedale Memorial Church, Grandma Dora was her sole companion, that is, until yesterday, when her biological mother, Dorothy Ella Thornton (called 'Dot' by Jeanna) arrived unexpectedly from France after receiving her child's "farewell letter". Dot was met with a cold and angry reception from Grandma Dora, the mother Dot resented most of Jeanna's life, convinced the grandmother stole her only child from after their short-custody agreement expired, presumably because Dot was unstable and didn't have "a pot or a window" for her daughter. The enmity between them was palpable.

Jeanna's carefully worded message crushed her mother. The missive was filled with accusations and judgments which sank dagger-like into Dot's guilty conscience. Despite her initial heartbreak, Dot knew her only child was in distress; she returned to the town she once vowed to never see again. When she arrived in hysterics, Jeanna, lay still asleep and confined by Posey restraints, which her mother found disconcerting. As Dot attempted to enter the quiet chamber, she was met by her own mother, Dora, who angrily attempted to bar the woman from entering the room. As she rose from the recliner, she hissed, "Well, well, my one and only prodigal daughter, Jeanna's long-lost mother! What the hell, Lord forgive me, are you doing here daughter!"

Dot replied haughtily, "Well, well, (sniffling and

dabbing her face with a handkerchief) hello to you too Mother! I'm here, like you to be with my only child" Jeanna sent this (waved the note in the air) scathing letter and I knew something had to be terribly wrong because we haven't talked in years! I knew I had to come immediately" (pauses, inhales dramatically and continues). "I went to the house and Miss Janie, your neighbor, told me what happened." Dot demanded tearfully, "How can you be call yourself a Christian and never bothered to contact me Mother? How could you be so nasty and so callous at a time like this? I'm her mother!" With those words, Dot burst into tears, pushed past her mother, entered the room and peered at the daughter she had not seen for more than eighteen years, and cried quietly as Jeanna, unware of her presence, slept.

Grandma Dora stood visibly beside herself while staring at her prodigal with perturbed annoyance over her reading glasses. Dot busied herself with settling in and ignored the glare. After she whispered a prayer, she then settled in the stiff blue chair, sniffling quietly as she arranged herself by the wardrobe closet. "Mother, I'm exhausted and I refuse to argue. I'm taking a nap". With those words, she fell into an exhausted slumber beside her daughter. The grandmother, nonplussed, stared blankly at Dot, then Jeanna, sighed "Lord have mercy", then returned to the where she read the Bible, until fatigue and sleepiness overtook her.

Perhaps it was the palpable tension between the warring mothers that stirred Jeanna from her transient rest. Facing the bright ceiling, still feeling acutely hung-over, her addled mind unexpectedly conjured myriad images of the failed suicide attempt. She remembered swallowing the Xanax™ pills with some expensive vodka, all while inhaling outrageously greasy vegetable tempura, which she loved, before disrobing and masturbating with her favorite vibrator. "Oh no!" she thought. Did she remove the toy before everything went dark? "Oh sh—, Lord forgive me' (Jeanna always asked God for forgiveness after cursing, a habit learned from Grandma Dora). Though her awareness was still vague, everything about the event regrettably converged upon" her memory, and Jeanna inwardly shrieked with humiliation. 'Sh--, sh--, sh-! Lord forgive me! I think I still had the Rabbit™ in me when I passed out!"

It was, in fact, found still buzzing, lodged between her heavy thighs, where it remained long after the overdose kicked in. Jeanna remembered she laid their butt-naked, and was obviously found in the same position, sprawled on the queen-sized bed like a drunken doll, her legs spread eagle, with badly chipped toenails, and hairy underarms (she stopped shaving after she set the suicide date). The perverse imageries of that night mortified her. That volunteer rescuers and Rosedale's local police saw Jeanna, one of the city's most respected lawyers in such a diminished state was unbearable. Facing her community and the constituents who depended upon her, was even worse! While it clearly would not have mattered if anyone saw her corpulent, **dead** body, she was <u>still alive</u>, and all her 'business' had been seen by the Rosedale officers, and emergency responders, many of whom she knew from high school and church.

For weeks, Jeanna planned, rearranged and over-scheduled her demise and was sure the deadly mixture of drugs and alcohol guaranteed eternal oblivion. "What happened? How and why didn't the deadly concoction work?" She could care less about the heroic efforts made to resuscitate her. She wanted to die, **damnit** (Lord forgive me)! No, Jeanna did not appreciate the round-the-clock vigils the Pastor conducted with members at church. Neither were the concerns of Jeanna's immediate family important. The pressing was "How in the world, if I survived the excruciating backlash of these toxic drugs lingering in my system, am I ever going to endure seeing my grandmother after this?" She could care less about her colleagues, haters who shamelessly vied for her vaunted position in the firm. They all hated Jeanna's seemingly meteoric rise in the agency which had been exacerbated by her aloof manner they mistook for arrogance. Grandma Dora was everything to her.

Besides, Jeanna had already sent off a letter of resignation weeks ago so there really was chance of going back. Not after this fiasco. What was worse, that small mocking voice chided, was that everyone by now had knowledge of Jeanna's well-publicized attempt at self-murder! The worst part of it all was her unbearably mortifying sense of exposure. Jeanna loathed anything which drew attention to her. She wasn't painfully shy, just relentlessly self-conscious and fastidious about her public persona. The cowardly refuge of death would have concealed Jeanna's apparent frailties, but there was no cover for her now, save the flimsy shield the hospital sheets offered. It would be inexorably agonizing to explain her "business" to folks and she resented the imminent intrusions and narrow judgments.

Even explaining her mental illness battle to Pastor James Wade, a devoted, but misguided shepherd who once told parishioners to "Pray the Cray away", instead of directing people to get (in some cases) badly needed psychiatric care, would be impossible, she imagined. Pastor Wade was a young but zealous preacher, brought up in the disciplines of the faith his grandfather Zechariah Wade entrusted to those willing to strictly adhere to "nothing but the Word". Psychology, cultural and social phenomena were not considered factors in illnesses, in his view, so all healing rested solely upon prayer, and, in the province and faith of the afflicted. Two Sundays ago, Jeanna's shepherd made intercession for Jeanna and other burdened souls at the church while accompanied by the elders. Pastor Wade offered prayer to all who were struggling with something they can't bear" and Jeanna joined the crowd standing at the altar.

She recalled the forlorn and self-conscious way she held herself erectly at the front of the church, with her knees knocking and her mind racing. Naturally, Jeanna's dress was unimpeachable; the pink St. John knit suit and matching Jimmy Choo's were complimented by Mikimoto pearls and a ring that adorned her manicured hands raised before the deacons and deaconesses of the church. It had been established by Jeanna's great-great-great-great grandfather, Elisha Wells Thornton , along with six leaders in the Rosedale community after Reconstruction; the original building, recognized as a historic landmark, sat adjacent to the new edifice Jeanna's and her family had attended for decades. A debate wavered within her soul about healing. "If I am truly healed do I continue taking my anti-anxiety medications? She thought about the possibility of faith healing and became filled with a mixture of hope and dejection.

She winced after the fervent minister called the church mothers to circle and pray out "that *filthy* demon spirit of heaviness", which oppressed

Jeanna for nearly two decades. The word *filthy* struck Jeanna's guilt-ridden conscience; if the demon was vile, and upon her, didn't that make her vile and filthy too? Would she be delivered at the same time from fornication and masturbation? These kind of musings often interrupted Jeanna's concentration, and were a trait of Dysthymia. With few exceptions, distracted thinking bedeviled Jeanna most of her young adult life, undermining the brilliance that shone through in the courtroom. She would often disrupt the unsolicited reveries by force, and, with frustration, but the meanderings seemed persistent more often than not.

Other intrusive contemplations were dismissed as Pastor Wade spoke in tongues, liberally spread oil on Jeanna's forehead and pressed his palm into her temple as if to brand her. Pressure and gravity moved Jeanna backwards, and the church members sounded a collective "Yes Lord!" as her fall appeared driven by the Spirit, not the heavy hand on her head. Jeanna lay there, in keeping with her church training, waiting for inordinate weightiness of her affliction to be removed, for what seemed an eternity. Then, she was helped to her feet by the nurses, and escorted back to the pew where her grandmother sat weeping. "How you feel Jeannie?" Grandma Dora asked hopefully. Unwilling to disappoint her beloved surrogate, Jeanna said, 'I feel fine Grandma, I really do', but the grandmother stared dubiously into Jeanna's tear- filled slate eyes. It didn't work; she still felt unclean, depressed, and persuaded that nothing would purge her soul but death.

By this time, Jeanna had already grown weary of battling often agonizing, invisible torments and depressed moods and she was worn down; the emotional exhaustion of the disorder was stifling. People had no idea what sometimes Herculean efforts were needed just to keep going some days, and, how nearly every minute of every day became an overbearing, numbing task. Her Life had become, Jeanna believed, painfully circumscribed by her illness. Not only this, Jeanna perceived her burdensomeness each time she gazed into the worry-wrinkled face of her grandmother. The constant sense of being "under someone's watch made Jeanna feel as oppressed as the girdles she wore to conceal her thickness. Keeping up the façade of stability, of togetherness demoralized Jeanna more than her condition.

When would it be acceptable for seemingly accomplished folks like Jeanna, to openly express their mighty inner struggles? Was a mentally ill person any less lovable, despite tending to fall apart when unknown triggers were activated? Most important, would she find love despite all her "issues"? She had dreams like most women and they seemed impossible, she believed, because of the affliction. Despairingly, Jeanna chose August 11 as the day to end the aching charade.

Now, laying there fully aware of the failed attempt, as well as the countless difficulties she faced upon her recovery, Jeanna wept silently and asked again, "Why, Lord, and HOW the hell, Lord forgive me, am I still alive?" Feelings of dismay, self-loathing, and astonishment were silenced by sharp throbbing in her head. Laying there brokenly, she flailed weakly, chanting, "NO, NO, NO" while crying silently. She allowed uninhibited imaginations to vie for her attention because she was literally tired.

The mind is amazingly adept at reminding humans of things that cannot be willed into oblivion. Central to well-being is the ability to create and store memories. Once the mind creates a memorial through that complex, miraculous process called *protein synthesis*, like matter, the history cannot be destroyed. Nothing could obliterate the traumas, rejections and disappointment Jeanna retained. They shaped the sadness, self-loathing and ultimately her decision to end her life. Their omnipresence bruised her fragile ego made her feel so powerless to escape them. For many battling Dysthymia, powerlessness, along with intangible feelings of despair, drives their decision to die.

Even with the crushing weight of Jeanna's predicament, deep down in her soul, beneath all the hellishness of the disease, Something held Jeanna's soul in the present. It was a force she dared not consider because she had a bone or two to pick with God. Jeanna had been taught to blindly accept as fate the diagnosis and complaints were discouraged. Like that old song "I Won't Complain" Jeanna was inculcated to believe she had no right to her anger, that afflictions came from God to teach her a lesson. "Well dang," she burst out furiously one day. "When the hell is this lesson over God?" Now, of course Jeanna now realized that illness was not from God, but rather the burden of humanity, the result untreated traumas, biochemistry and, in some cases, generational predisposition. Truthfully, she knew that God was no fairy and that healing, though "the children's bread" as Pastor said, required the cooperation of the afflicted; she had never been willing to submit to any prescriptive for her health.

But she so angry and wanted to scream violently, but Grandma Dora's spirit nearby quelled her discomfiture. Like a petulant child she ignored His presence in her room. God, in all of His Holiness, Who visited the afflicted in heaven or in hell, was an unnerving Judge to Jeanna. She hadn't felt the peace and warmth of His Presence in years. Still, His omniscience, even in a room adjacent to the psychiatric ward, was undeniable. Unworthy tears flowed, but she resented His intervention.

Timorously she asked, "If You love me, God and I have a free-will, then why didn't You let me die? What happened to Fu—ing, Lord please forgive me, MY Free Will!" Silence answered. Exasperation, penitence, and apprehension about a future she believed was certain to perpetuate despondency and emotional anguish attacked her mind. But she could not deny He was still present. His Love was unavoidable. She knew it. Despite His ubiquity, hateful despair, that powerful demon, loitered impudently, like an unwanted guest Jeanna felt powerless to evict. The only consolation was her awareness of Grandma Dora's steady presence. But, how would she console the matriarch of the remaining Thornton family, especially in this wretched state? Jeanna remembered guiltily that she had sworn to Grandma Dora's face that she would do nothing to harm herself just days ago.

Just hours before Jeanna stirred from unconsciousness, the doctors explained to her anxious kin that while the medicine revived her autonomic functions like breathing, Jeanna would have to wake up on her own, as her will to die may outweigh everyone's hope for her to live on. He also told them how strongly the mind can drive people to carry out detrimental or affirming choices. Life or death rested wholly on Jeanna's will. Grandma Dora agreed with the prognosis and told the psychiatrist, "My grandchild may still be fighting to die Doctor, and you have done all you can, but God has a plan she can't stop! My Jeanna knew what she was doing; suicide is not an accident; my baby made a planned choice, and all we can do now is pray." Grandma Dora knew from that Sunday service that Jeanna seemed to have lost hope.

Hope, in her mind, was the core of all human endurance. It's what helped her ancestors overcome the evils of slavery and set up prosperous settlements in Rosedale and other towns. It was the engine of Faith. But people battling the chronic depressed moods that characterize Dysthymia sometimes lose their ability to see light at the end of the tunnel. Depression invoked what doctors call "primitive" and "narrow' thinking that does not consider future possibilities because the pain of NOW consumes everything, as it did for Jeanna. Soon, negativity takes on "a life of its own", as a self-fulfilling prophecy. One proverb says, "As a man thinks in his heart, so is he" and, in the case of Dysthymia, those pernicious negative thoughts become more powerful than reality itself.

Jeanna was so controlled by destructive inner predictions about her future that everything looked bleak. She epitomized what she had internalized-despondency. Her feelings of hopelessness were magnified all the core beliefs she had already internalized unconsciously since childhood, and that fragile state was a perfect storm for her down-spiral. The old saints in church used say things like "the devil had a plan". Now that she was older, it seemed that Satan's devices were destined for her mental crisis. Mental traps are a perfect set up. To be convinced that life is less valuable than death, and to live as if this lie were true, made the victim his/her own accuser as well. Jeanna lost strength to withstand these diabolical mental assaults; her suicide attempt, Grandma Dora declared, was Jeanna's surrender to the enemy of her mind. She wasn't alone but no one in the family dared examine the causalities of the disease plaguing the clan. Having done all, she thought she could do to heal, the crush of each failed attempt hastened Jeanna's conclusion that, at 43, she was already damaged and beyond repair or hope.

Also, Jeanna was her severest critic, and delivered merciless self-judgments, so she found it easy to demonize herself. Her balanced reasoning had already been obscured by seed of self-hatred planted in her childhood. People, like Jeanna, who want to escape pain-filled life experiences, who find themselves thwarted at every attempt at achieving a "normal" life, and mainstream dreams like marriage and children, firmly hang their defeats on their own heads. Deferred hope makes the heart heavy, and, for depressed persons, hope becomes nonexistent making "light at the end of the tunnel" messages cruel ridicules. Jeanna's discouragement felt like the dismay a blind person must feel when an artist holds a picture up to their face, and hopes he can somehow interpret it's meaning. At the time of Jeanna's self-immolation, a heavy shroud of despondency so overweighed every sphere of her life that fought to obliterate its presence by annihilating herself.

After the failed effort, many of Jeanna's church members, some probably laden by their own inner conflicts, were baffled and feared that some unknown and wicked spiritual force drove Jeanna's illness. Several parishioners acted like the chronic disorder was somehow, a highly contagious plague. Others dreaded even speaking of Jeanna's malady, as if such utterances were a leprous. The church's ignorance about Dysthymia was sustained as much by fear as mispronunciations. Some called it "*Thymena*", (a diseased herb), while others said it was called *"This-time-is-up"*, (signaling perhaps it's deadly nature). For other uninformed souls, Jeanna was a woman stricken of the **devil**, not someone fighting a syndrome that was part biochemical, part predisposition, and part self-driven.

Thankfully, there were a few brave soldiers who stood watch in prayer vigils as they were exhorted by Grandma Dora. They kept praying, even when advised that Jeanna could remain in a comatose state. Choruses of "Amends" and "Yes Lord's" filled the waiting room at the church matron's urgings. Two hours after those prayers, Jeanna opened her slate grey eyes, blinking repeatedly, chest heaving as she gulped for air. Though disoriented, petrified, and, angry with herself and God, Jeanna sensed His Spirit had beckoned her return to the land of the living, where nothing had changed. In fact, things were worse. Far worse. Sure, God was here, but so was the absurd nausea, and, worse, a crippling headache that felt like a hammer bashing her brain.

Still, nothing compared with the raw self-recrimination Jeanna now experienced with her grandmother sitting nearby. Shame washed over her in relentless waves. Grandma Dora's Youth Dew cologne mixed with the cold air, and her warm pale right hand, gnarled by rheumatoid arthritis, clasped Jeanna's left shoulder to signal her presence. The grip felt like a mother desperately holding on to her only child for dear life. Grandma Dora snored with a quiet hum that echoed in the smallish room. She was a fair-skinned, diminutive, but powerful woman, who could easily pass for a Caucasian, but was a proud "Rosedale Negro" (her term) who advocated for her dark grandchild all of her life. Grandma Dora rested sideways in the uncomfortable-looking blue lounger next to Jeanna's bed, her well-worn, ever-present King James Bible nearby.

Repressed tears poured from Jeanna's ducts, while intense sickness made her stomach lurch like the precipitous drop of a rollercoaster, and caught Jeanna's breath. Rumbling nausea threatened to expel remnants of the poisons still in her system, but Jeanna clenched her stomach muscles and her fists to push the bile down. Slowly, after several minutes, she ventured to open her eyes; diplopia doubled her vision of everything in the room, magnifying its blinding brightness. Quickly and in fear, she shut her eyes quickly to stop the intense light from burning through her hypersensitive irises. Jeanna hated brightness; It grieved her soul. Brightness was an accursed thing to people who, like Jeanna, preferred to battle their depressed moods under the veil of darkness. Maybe it helped them to avoid the illusory hope that light produced, or, maybe blackness helped others find fleeting faith in the peace darkness appeared to offer.

In Jeanna's case, the dark rooms in her home hid the mirrors she detested. this practice of self-avoidance triggered Jeanna's eventual and complete self- detachment, which, over time, made her plan for self-murder less horrifying to conceive. Unfortunately, her current ward was full of the pungent force of brightness, which overwhelmed Jeanna's already frazzled senses with the impression of nakedness that had nothing to do with her flimsy bed coverings. Along with the bright lamps, a raucous tumult in Jeanna's belly seemed magnified by the fluorescent lamps above her head post To calm the incessant dizziness whirling around her, Jeanna sealed her lids' as tears forcefully rose and spilled onto her cheeks . When she attempted to move her left arm to wipe her face, the Posey restraints strapped on her tender wrists and ankles restrained the effort.

Bitterness mingled with heartache, as she realized how vulnerable and defenseless she was in that hospital bed. Here she was, a celebrated lawyer degenerated into a psychiatric ward patient covered only by a backless gown, controlled by Velcro-straps attached to a plastic mattress adorned with thin white sheets, and a blue blanket. Worse than this was the diaper that moved as she lifted her midsection to get comfortable. A twin-sized, regulation mattress squeaked with her actions, so she gave up, fearful of awakening the family matriarch. Instead, she whimpered quietly, numbed by the prospect of enduring Grandma Dora's cross-examination more than anything, or, anyone else, including her colleagues. What could be said to console to the woman she confided her most scandalous thoughts and hidden sins, except this heinous one? How could anything comfort her staunchest advocate whom she lied to in church two weeks ago? This woman defended Jeanna as ferociously as a lioness defends her cubs. The quandary made her long for escape into nothingness, headfirst, back into a blissful abyss of coma.

She could endure anything but that unforgettable look of sorrow she had seen more than once on her surrogate mother's face. What made things worse was that she would probably still be immobilized, lying face-up, arms and legs spread eagle, in the damn agonizingly bright cell of a room! Jeanna blinked salt water back quickly, eyes still shut, fearful that her eyes were permanently damaged by her drug overdose. She laid there still as the night, listening and crying.

2- "CONTEMPLATION"

As the fluorescent lamp buzzed above Jeanna's head, it beamed penetrating rays of light that bore down on her sealed eyelids, prying them open. Her brief glimpse of the room revealed piles of unread greeting cards, sinking balloons, and two sad, dying floral arrangements; all of the items sat clogging the windowpane and the bedside table occupying the funereal, beige-colored room. The light brown shade evoked stark plainness and boredom. Cold institutional tile flooring shone dully beneath the small unit's bleak furnishings, and a single window vista exposed peeling, cracked tar roofs, families of pigeons, and the detritus left behind, presumably by hospital workers. Utilitarian curtains hung dejectedly beside the plywood wardrobe.

The area was depressingly lackluster; under Jeanna's still-unsteady vision, the pathetic scenery frighteningly expanded and contracted. A slight turn alarmed the polyurethane mattress, which squealed noisily. Grandma Dora snorted, as if her sleep was interrupted and Jeanna froze while her sickness was further roused. Rolling waves of queasiness crested in her esophagus; Jeanna turned her face as she choked back salty spittle and inhaled slowly to avert queasiness, sealing her eyes to squeeze out the sun's rays. She considered her present state an imprisonment worse than her mental illness. She felt ensnared in the lamp's mocking, ubiquitous torture, and longed for the cover of darkness which disguised her self-flagellation.

Her aversion to brightness had infiltrated every facet of her existence, including work, where she donned shades at the office purportedly to shelter her eyes from the office lighting, but really, she hated the knowing gazes of her colleagues. Jeanna believed, like most people with mental illness, that EVERYONE knew she struggled, and she worked hard to disprove their assumptions.

Crippling social anxiety, and unreasonable mistrust of her associates drove many of Jeanna's sometimes irrational decisions, and her social aloofness, which was both a comfort and a source of shame. Living alone since college enabled Jeanna to abscond scrutiny and accountability, which empowered her unhealthy coping skills. They helped to masked Jeanna's feelings of penetrating loneliness and self-disappointment from everyone. Now, she worried that all of her frailties were on excruciating public display and the realization made Jeanna squirm under the bedcovers.

To Jeanna, appearance was everything, and her now - public exposure was beyond humiliating. Everyone - the first responders, the police, her family, exes, nosey-a--, Lord forgive me, jealous neighbors, her tenants, that cheating lying mofo Duray, her coworkers, Pastor Wade, probably all the choir members, and, oh my God! The list was endless. She was sure most of Rosedale was now aware that Jeanna Rose Audrey Thornton, while in the throes of the Dysthymia that rendered her acutely and relentlessly despondent last week, tried to commit suicide with a lethal concoction of Russian vodka, Xanax and artery-clogging tempura. Would her Pharisaical judges would comprehend how painful it was to be entrenched in perpetual singlehood, at a time when her sex drive was at its agonizing peak? How many would understand that she managed her increasingly depressed moods with sex and food? Could anyone of them empathize with a professional woman, whose means of managing stress involved compulsive masturbation everyday with all kinds of experimental implements, including the vacuum hose, under the cloak of darkness? God forbid anyone discovered or extensive sex toy collection, or, learn that each Friday in court, Jeanna escaped her mundane and cloistered life by marathon viewings of XXX-porn while pleasing herself?

Worse would be public knowledge about Jeanna's relationship with Duray Meekins, the 22-year old, ex-convict who subsisted on SSI-D Disability Insurance, and lived like a trifling leech between his mama's house and his baby mama's subsidized apartment. He was a shameless, sociopathic fraud, who made lots of empty promises Jeanna sopped up like a fool, but my God, they had the best sex ever and that mattered a lot to her at the time, especially since it helped her cope with her sad moods, until she got pregnant. Despite his treachery, Jeanna knew she had a strong soul tie to him through their intimacy that was not easily broken. Her connection, Pastor Wade explained after her half – confession (she never told his age) last month, was powerful; she treated the young man as if her were her husband, not her partner in sin and their separation felt like a messy divorce.

Fornication, for many single sexually-deprived men and women, was a powerful and comforting means of satisfaction. Jeanna always reasoned that sex hurt no one, but deep inside, she knew the habit informed every decision in her life. At work, she thought of ways to pleasure herself, despite her relationship with Duray. Her otherwise empty life found its purpose in her mantra, "I don't have a man, or child at home, so Im'ma do me"; intercourse was part big part of her doing. Still, Jeanna remained desperately sad within, and her habit, like all drugs, no longer offered the high it first produced; now it turned on her, leaving her empty like a spurned lover. She felt horny strangely enough, as she lay prone, tied, and filled with guilt. The uncovering was inescapable, and she was crushed by an awareness that she, a public figure, brought such unseemly publicity upon herself.

All, including her once cherished communion with God, seemed lost. For some time, Jeanna had been a faltering church-goer constrained primarily by the Thornton family's religious traditions. Self-recrimination would cripple her if she missed service. She'd be so guilt-ridden that repentance and self-flogging would have preceded her Sunday's routine. The altar call beckoned her nearly every week, along with other penitents. Still, Jeanna could not imagine life without her sexual fetishes, despite her soul's torment. Not only were they addictive, but she loved feeling short-lived control and contentment. Her public self was the epitome of decorum because keeping up appearances, was "de riguer" In Rosedale. No one dared to bring shame to the family name by defecting from religious observances, even if the devotion was hollow pageantry.

Besides this, Jeanna believed church was her last defense against the disease, which rendered her often and emotionally exhausted. Despite her wavering faith, she believed the elders, anointed oils, prayers, supplication, bargaining, vows and every other possible entreaty one could make to a seemingly implacable God, kept the demons at bay. She knew her church attendance was a hollow ritual, a burdensome Sunday charade she carried on for her grandmother's sake. Inwardly, she resented God, His unbending laws, and His judgment. She felt betrayed by the empty promises of Psalm 23 ('When have you comforted me?' she argued), and His inexcusable silence. "Why am I still single God?'; No answer. 'I would have bene a great wife and mother so why have You deprived me of my dream?' More silence, all made worse by the empty platitudes from the good-intentioned church members who exhorted, "Remember all things work together for the good", or "God knows what you can bear Jeanna".

She wanted to scream at these bamboozled souls, 'Please Shut the hell up with those empty answers! My life f—ing hurts like hell, and all you can say is that!' Instead, Jeanna often smiled politely, said "Amen", and walk away, enraged. Her fury, she didn't realize, left unsatisfied, turned into the wrath which demanded a penalty, even from the victim. The well-masked vehemence she carried in her soul became so deep-seated that, like a traitor, it turned rabidly upon her and, instead of looking outside of her agony, everything burned within. Combined with her Dysthymia disorder, the consequences were lethal. At her lowest of despair she reasoned that death was the only alternative to the protracted grief carried angrily for months, then years. She set the date for her demise and went about the important task of getting her affairs in order.

Her first and most important task was releasing all the trespassers of the debts they owed. Jeanna's high sense of fairness required people to reap what they had sown in her life, and so she appointed herself the sole arbiter of the justice they deserved. With eagle eye sharpness, Jeanna recollected the hurts she had collected over the year like prizes. Thirty-one offenders were carefully listed on the spreadsheet; each was to have vengeance meted out to them after Jeanna crossed over. From grade school, to her rites of passage through college and career, Jeanna chronicled those she deemed most contemptuous and deserving of her self-righteous retribution. Pain-filled memories emerged and multiplied her already implacable 'sorrowfulness', a term Grandma Dora coined when Jeanna was a child.

Each was scheduled to receive meticulously drafted missives the day AFTER she perished; unfortunately, she survived her self-immolation and knew she would have to face them. While crafting her retaliation, Jeanna reasoned, "Oh well, they deserve everything coming to them", which assuaged her alarm, but foreboding thoughts amplified as she now remembered the names. After compiling the "hit list", Jeanna's subconscious warned her, 'Girl, it's been years since these incidents, so why are you doing this?' Why had Jeanna preserved such pain-filled memories like cherished heirlooms all these years? It was exhausting to carefully memorialize wrongdoings she suffered from others, but her unforgiveness goaded her ii-advised plan forward.

The first letter was mailed to the Rosedale School Board to warn them about Roy Singleton, Jeanna's childhood "pretend uncle" who molested her when she was nine. He absconded the wrath of the Thornton's by leaving town under the cover of night, returning years later to teach math at her former middle school. She advised the School Board of the unsubstantiated crimes he committed, confident the Bible-thumping members would raise Holy hell and remove the pedophile from his post.

With fervent relish, Reginald Ferguson, the sadistic bully from Rosedale High School who called her "Blackie", "Monkey" and other horribly derogatory names throughout high school, was 'outted'. His attacks back then reinforced Jeanna's acute feelings of inferiority, and made her loathe her dark skin. He used Jeanna as his personal scapegoat while disguising his confused sexuality. She was vindicated upon learning that her tormentor, though married with children, was corresponding with Donte Lawson, an openly gay associate on her job. She emailed the lewd photos Reginald sent to Donte under the hashtag #MrBigStuff to Pastor Wade and to wife, savoring bittersweet revenge as she pressed the send button. Pastor Wade was one of the most homophobic males she had ever met and she knew he would excoriate Reginald.

As Jeanna's vengefulness continued, she became disquieted about the magnitude of her deep-rooted hostility, and, realized that some of the transgressions were, in hindsight, petty, but she remained nonetheless fixated on vengeance, and ignored morality. The pause strengthened Jeanna's resolve to die as she pitifully reasoned, 'I can't look back now, after doing all of this', then, calmly, stoically, with unwavering determination published her last will and testaments, examining the list obsessively to ensure that not one stone of offense remained unturned. It was exhausting, but strangely exhilarating at the same time. She was assailed by her conscience during the exercises, reminded by the Spirit that 'Love doesn't remember when others do it wrong Jeanna', and "Love suffers long and is kind, Jeanna.

Appeals to moral convictions were rebutted with, "Love also says an eye for an eye", and the vendetta continued. Jeanna's mother, Dot would get her letter one week before her demise. She wanted to be long gone when the letter arrived in Bordeaux, France. Ironically, Dot received it the day after Jeanna ingested the lethal dose of pills and liquor. Since the concoction failed, Jeanna reckoned she would have to face the consequences of her somehow botched scheme, or, develop another suicide plan. The restraints were clearly a barrier to that latter option; she forlornly acknowledged. Worse were the disquieting tortures ravaging her body. Her victims, like ghosts of holidays passed, randomly flashed before Jeanna in a parade of accusation.

First, there was Dorrance Poe (light-skinned hoe who stole her first love; fronting and broke, facing foreclosure), Vincent Magee (Defense lawyer who padded cases), Judge Pendleton (drug addict; KKK member), Viola Smith (choir member, bully and lesbian), Jessica Robinson (gym class tormentor; facing wire fraud charges), Harold Williamson (peeping Tom, stalker; had sex with Judge Paul Smith), Dee Morse (harassed Jeanna for being dark; stealing from law firm), Elfreda Hughes (Chemistry teacher; graded blacks poorly; hiding contagious disease from colleagues at Rosedale High) Judge Paul Smith, a racist homophobe dating a Black man). Jeanna redressed her issues with The Sphinx Social Club (filed ACLU complaint), the staff at Klein's Department store (letter to NAACP), the thoroughly uncouth and conceited Elect First Lady of Rosedale Memorial Church (Horrible body odor; rancid breath), and to George Spivey (married a former stripper).

Then, she squared off with Leon Cortes (who reneged on his promise to take her to the junior prom if she performed fellatio behind the football stand (she obliged more than once; 'his penis is the size of a child's' she posted on social media). Then, there was the note to Lisa Humphries (cruel high school prom queen, now a three hundred pound mother of five; your husband is cheating with your best friend), Deacon Harold and his wife Audrey (serve at church; saw you shopping after the church offering went missing), a fiery memo to Linda Ragsdale's husband Edward (leaving for work, but fired weeks ago), Elaine Brooks (dating Deloris Burch), Deloris Burch (dating Elaine Brooks and Edward Ragsdale), Aretha Moore (lesbian; filed EEOC complaint against Jeanna; also padding criminal cases), Estelle Moton (mean; grating church organist; addicted to opiates), Dorcas Findley (Black, trying to pass as white), as well as Elisa White (cheating wife), and Floyd Estes (Deacon; raging alcoholic; beats wife every Sunday).

Final communications were sent to James Muse (unregistered Megan's Law offender), to Cecily Rhone (runs a brothel), to Maria Stevenson (mean shrew sells her painkillers), to Leslene Foster (choir leader and number runner), to Edith Jones (stole boyfriend at college; falsified credentials for job at law firm), to Lorrene Polk, (kleptomaniac and gossip), to Mr. Jonas Perkins (courting Grandma Dora, cheating on her), to her father Nathaniel Graves (alcoholic, dead-beat father) and of course, Duray Meekin's baby mama Tashika (your baby daddy is my "tenderoni boo"), and finally, to Dot (her trifling, absentee mother). The reverie stopped there. 'Oh my God, what about all the people I attacked? What am I going to say to all of them? If Jeanna survived the harrowing discomfort of the hangover, she knew the victims would inevitably have to be met, but none of these impending clashes were as distressing as coming to terms with Dorothy Louise Thornton.

With that thought, Jeanna became despondently

engrossed with fear; in a silent panic, she begged, 'Lord, I can't! can't face these folks, especially HER'. THAT issue had to be deferred as long as she could bear her agony. Jeanna was grown, but a childlike fear and cowardice engrossed her. Paralyzed with dread, Jeanna hoped and prayed to the God she barely trusted for sleep. Vainly, Jeanna hoped the sounds loudly resonating from the medical equipment and tubes would lull her into obliviousness, but the clamors made that goal an absurd fantasy. The racket was nerve-wracking!

Clattering merged with her racing thoughts and magnified Jeanna's disquiet. She wanted to scream like a lunatic, but her fat, foreign tongue paralyzed her larynx, and the restraints immobilized her impulses. Plus, she still feared her grandmother's judgment. Echoing clamors ricocheted against the ward's bedroom walls, forbidding slumber. 'I'm screwed! I can't sleep and my stomach is torturing me!' She wailed quietly, and tensed her abdomen as something akin to seasickness raged in her belly.

The pain was indescribable.

Clenching her fists, she willed the storm to calm and hung on. Seconds stretched, it seemed, into eternity as Jeanna became more alert with each commotion. Shrill hums syncopated her grandmother's snorts, worsening the constant sounding in Jeanna's head. Feeling powerless to do anything but arch her back and yank weakly on the guardrails, Jeanna slumped with a soft thud on the pillow. Grandma Dora's wheezing subsided and Jeanna peeked slowly, fearing her eyes; she quickly peered askance at the tiny figure resting quietly as ever in the chair. Relieved but sullen, she strained to rest, but remained alerted by the idea that, barring complete organ failure, which, considering her current agony, seemed quite possible, she would not only deal with thirty victims targeted in her vindictive dispatches, but she would also confront the greatest source of her malcontent – Dot, whom she imagined still overseas and unaware of her condition. Stifled sobbing turned into nearhiccupping and another bout of sickness followed.

After inhaling unsteadily, Jeanna compressed her eyes and, by sheer willpower, she held the intense sickness at bay. Spasms, her system's effort to expel the foreign elements attacking her gut, shook her violently; her legs throbbed with prickly stinging. 'This is like death' she surmised. Still high, Jeanna's mind raced with arbitrary, disordered, and perverse visions, as an inexplicable giddiness overtook her; part hangover, part hallucination, and then, Jeanna imagined the gates of heaven were opening as a foreign scent grazed her nostrils. She wretched again, and fought with all her might to suppress the reflexes driving her to heave. Grandma Dora stirred from her sleep. Jeanna froze in the bed, and shifted her weight towards the window in the room, near the armoire. After taking painstakingly slow breaths to stave off another spasm of nausea, her body submitted, and the vomiting subsided.

At the same time, as calm arose, a sweet

fragrance wafted, then landed gently, like a petal on Jeanna's nose. She strained to distinguish the calming notes in the perfume, her curiosity goading her to look in direction of the seemingly divine bouquet. Her heart skipped, then plummeted. A chilling sensation scaled her right side. The Chanel purse was a giveaway; she had it neatly tucked in the recliner situated beside the wardrobe. Dot sat asleep, petite as ever, her pale complexion flawless. She was the arbiter of impeccable fashion, with her stockinged feet curled up daintily beneath the flimsy covers. Dot preferred the finest hand-crafted perfumes, the best clothes, food, things and this fragrance was filled with soft notes of floral, which calmed Jeanna's overloaded senses. Incredulity, excited fear, then rage captivated her foggy mind.

Still dazed, she wondered what the hell, Lord forgive her, was Dot, her long-absent mother doing here, after eighteen m%%erf#@##in 'Lord please forgive me' years? Why had she come at a time like this, when Jeanna was in such a wretched state, and, unbelievably, still alive? The letter, viciously worded, was to have been Jeanna's swan song to the woman she dutifully loved, and reviled. "Oh my God, that letter was so malicious!" Jeanna recoiled unconsciously. The missive was replete with contemptuous expletives, and had been judiciously composed, edited twice, and, express-mailed to some pretentious estate in Bordeaux, France her mother shared with that vile paramour, Jerome LaPierre. In France, it was reported, Dot reinvented herself, obliterating her identity as the extravagant daughter of a teenage mother from Rosedale, to a cosmopolitan, French-speaking socialite who, with the blessing of her well-heeled benefactor, had become a fixture in the arts society. A gifted dancer, Dot's thwarted ambitions were satisfied by her patronage of the artist societies there.

Jeanna remembered how Dot not only renounced her US citizenship, but also shamefully exploited her Eurocentric features to disguise her African ancestry, it was said. Of course, like most

"IncogNegroes" (as Grandma Dora categorized them), Dot repudiated claims by her family that she was "passing", but instead, reasoned obliquely that her 'colorblindness' was a revelation received from the spirits of her White ancestors, whose blood mingled with Georgia's slaves. She refused to renounce her whiteness; instead, Dot developed ways to seamlessly evade the ugly questions of her ethnicity. She rationalized these questions mattered only in racist America, not Europe, (who exported slaveholders to America). Her disavowals grieved and startled both of her parents, who were staunch advocates of ethnic pride. They feared their daughter's self-abnegation would cause her to ultimately abandon all ties to "American issues", including her only child, Jeanna, her dark-skinned beauty they loved. They knew Jeanna struggled mightily because of Rosedale's "color problem".

As feared, Dot left, unexpectedly eighteen years ago, despite knowing her daughter was graduating in less than two months as the senior class valedictorian from Rosedale High School. Dot said she had to follow Jerome to France, or, wherever he wished.   She wholly surrendered herself to his patronage and control.

3 – "DOT DEAREST"

When Dorothy Thornton was eighteen, she met Jerome LaPierre at the diner across from his corporate offices, where she worked as a waitress. The job funded her aspirational lifestyle of high-end fashion, and fine-dining in the studio apartment she shared with her best friend, and Jeanna's godmother, Sharon until she was courted by LaPierre. Since childhood, Dot fantasized about a jet-set life for her child that mirrored the luxurious images depicted in her mother's Jet and Ebony magazines. The path to those means, she learned, was far more difficult with no formal education. While Jeanna's grandmother saw to it that her charge finished high school, and even pushed Dot to get post-secondary education, Dot was more assured that her Eurocentric features and appealing figure were the keys to her upward mobility.

Moreover, she chafed under her mother's domineering and controlling manner. Grandma Dora's authority with Dot's only child, caused deep-seated resentment in Dot's heart, especially after her ties to

Jeanna's father, Nathaniel Jones, were severed after threats from the Thornton's, and vilification by most of the close-knit Rosedale community. Nathaniel absconded to Atlanta, Georgia after Grandma Dora threatened the college freshman with criminal charges for "raping an innocent child". The truth is, though five years her senior, Nathaniel and Dot believed they were in love, and pledged devotion to one another. Consensual intercourse led to Dot's unplanned pregnancy but Nathaniel pledged his devotion before her family to no avail, and he departed Rosedale under a cloud of controversy and with a broken heart. Soon thereafter, his family retreated to their native Chicago and, fearing for their only son, forbade Nathaniel to have further contact with Dot or his child.

Dot demanded her mother return the child when she prepared to move out, but Grandma Dora refused, and produced the legal custody papers Dorothy signed as an adolescent, when she was confident her mother would release Jeanna to her care after she reached the age of majority. "When you are stable and not running behind men in the streets, I will release your child from my custody, as long as you have a steady job and can provide for her without laying on your back" Jeanna's grandmother demanded. Intimidated and angry, Dot retreated, and vowed to get a stable situation for her and the child. After several failed relationships, and missed opportunities to advance her station in life, Dot considered Jerome LaPierre to be her ticket to upward mobility and a stable life for Jeanna. He seemed to offer Dot security she had not known since her own unstable childhood with her parents.

The French-born man was rich, handsome, of slight build, and balding in that way that required full surrender to baldness, which his vanity refused. The tuft of hair was unsightly but he cherished it clearly. Though undersized for a male, Jerome carried himself with such pompous self-importance that people overlooked this shortcoming. Dot learned much later that LaPierre was an impotent, narcissistic, perversely conniving short man seventeen years her senior. Desperately socially ambitious, the unconfirmed aristocrat posed as a venture capitalist, specializing in hedge funds. His scheme garnered unwanted oversight from the Federal Trade Commission years before he retreated to Europe with Dot. Naturally he played upon the petite, voluptuous young adult's low self-esteem and her naiveté, courting her with high-end shopping, fine dining and the promise of more, if she allowed him to cultivate her for high-society.

Desperate for entre into the life promised by the shrewd manipulator, and hoping to use his largesse to regain custody of her child, Dot accepted his advances and moved to his rented penthouse in exclusive Buckhead, knowing little to nothing about the enigmatic male. Dot's mother reviled the older man, calling him a "pervert". The ingénue learned painfully the extent of LaPierre's perversions over the course of their eighteen years together, especially his peculiar appetite for sex because of his impotence. Jerome explained his flagrant infidelity on his unique need for stimulation that included ménage a trio, role-playing and bondage. Before decamping to France Jerome also developed a peculiar fascination with Jeanna's flawless dark skin, her grey eyes and heavy curly hair which starkly contrasted Dot's pallid coloring and nearly straight texture.

LaPierre's attentions made Jeanna excruciatingly self-conscious, especially when he began to surreptitiously graze her arms and face in gestures he passed as affection. At twelve, Jeanna loved wearing her long hair loosely, believing falsely that it was her most attractive feature. She knew girls envied her locks, so she paraded her asset proudly. Jerome's fetishes apparently included Jeanna's hair too, and one day, while she visited, Jerome begged sneakily to touch Jeanna's lose curls after her mother ran to the store. Jeanna recalled his wrinkly tanned and stubbly fingers going through her locks, and then, down to her shirt. She jumped in fear, and turned around confused, facing the pedophile. She asked Jerome what he was doing and was shocked to see his pants dropped to his ankles, exposing his disgusting pink organ.

She backed away in disgust, closing her eyes, as

Jerome told her not to fear, that he would never harm her, and would be very good to her mother, and not put her in the streets if Jeanna was nice and showed her breasts. Jeanna, fearful for her mother's well-being, and desperate to continue having visits with her, complied and began to raise her shirt slowly, as shame filled her mind. Jerome's breathing became almost hoarse and Jeanna was dizzy with terror. Suddenly, the front door slammed with a jolt, and La Pierre pulled his trousers to cover himself. Dot called for Jeanna to come see her spoils from shopping

. Jeanna, eyes downcast, fixed her clothes as she backed out of Jerome's office quickly and closed the door. Tears streamed down her cheeks as she ran to her mother, and blurted the incident between her and the Frenchman. Despite Jeanna's descriptive details about his flaccid, uncircumcised genitalia, Dot was 'confused' she said, by Jerome's blubbering vehement denial, that was followed, days later, by a 5-carat diamond engagement ring. Dot suddenly became uncertain about the crime and called it a 'terrible misunderstanding'. Grandma Dora, incensed, picked Jeanna up hours later and asked her daughter, "Are you believing the word of that filthy child molester over your flesh and blood?" Speechless, Dot stood pleading for Jeanna to understand things children never apprehend about adults, and was then whisked from the penthouse after getting all of her belongings.

As Jeanna packed the car, Grandma Dora roundly threatened the shrinking perpetrator, who stood with Dot denying the allegations. Jeanna was forbidden to return to her mother as long as she stayed with a child molester. Dot stayed and Jeanna never returned. She was stung by her mother's allegiance to the man, and dismissed Dot's increasingly empty promises made during their surreptitious communications, (as all her activities were monitored by Jerome). She doubted her mother's empty assertions and plainly told her so one day. Guilt-ridden, Dot appealed to Jeanna's unwavering love when she was forced to break promises spoken hastily out of Jerome's hearing.

Dot longed for, and cherished the moments she stole with Jeanna when Jerome was working, greedily hugging her daughter, and hurriedly conversing before leaving the child to prepare meals for her benefactor before he arrived home. For years, Dot remained indebted to the dilettante, whom, she discovered later, was still married, but legally separated for several years from his wealthy and well-connected wife, who resided in Paris near Champs-Elysees with their three adult children. When confronted, Jerome irritably told Jeanna it was 'complicated' and she, obtuse as ever, remained blindly loyal to the scoundrel.

She stayed even when he faced criminal indictments for racketeering and mail-fraud. When LaPierre absconded to Bordeaux to avoid prosecution, Dot followed blithely. Under obscure terms of diplomatic immunity, Jerome avoided extradition, but was banned from ever returning to the U.S. Dot was heartbroken when her mother refused to send the granddaughter to France. 'With the man you let almost rape your child? Over my dead body!' she said. Jeanna remained in Rosedale until she left for Howard University in Washington, D.C. and Harvard in Cambridge, Massachusetts, returning to Rosedale to join the law firm owned by her mentor from her undergraduate alma mater. Meanwhile, despite the abuses she experienced with Jerome, Dot never returned to the Rosedale, even when her beloved grandmother, Luvenia Thornton, who raised her, died and yet, here she was, unexpectedly asleep beside her daughter.

As for her mother's first love and Jeanna's progenitor, Nathaniel Lewis Jones, Jeanna grew up knowing very little about native son from Chicago, whose family moved to Rosedale when he was three, except that he was a tall, handsome, charcoal-colored man with thin lips, brilliant teeth, and a mole near his chin just like his daughter. Nate, as he was known, was initially misled by Dot, who was so enamored of the church percussionist that she lied, and said she was nearly eighteen when, in fact she was two weeks' shy of her fourteenth birthday. Nate was apparently taken by Dot's seeming maturity and a brief, secret courtship followed, until Deacon Nixon discovered them not praying in the church's supply closet.

Both families were convened and Dot's deception and pregnancy were uncovered, much to the dismay of Nathaniel and his family who intended for their only son to attend Morehouse in the fall like his father, and then join the family's retail businesses in town. Dot's mother accused the young man of rape and threatened to file charges if the two connected again. At Grandma Dora's bidding, all ties with the Jones family were severed after Nathaniel was dispatched to relatives in Marietta, Georgia before school started. Dot was sequestered at her mother's home until she delivered Jeanna on July 15, 1972. The Jones family, who attended Rosedale Memorial Church like many families in town, were incensed by the grandmother's bullying and refused to acknowledge Jeanna, who was the spitting image of her father.

Grandma Dora appealed to Senior Pastor Wade

to ask the Jones' to financially support the child since they were well-off, and they refused, blaming Dot for 'trying to trap their good son'. By default, that dislike was transferred to their son's offspring. Jeanna remembered their unveiled hostility towards her when she was as a child. Not knowing the family story left the child no choice but to conclude that she was rejected because she was disliked and unlovable. Without any evidence to debunk her childhood reasoning, Jeanna internalized poor self- esteem, and over time, she developed self-preserving defense mechanisms which made her acutely sensitive to rejection, perceived or

real. Without Dot or her father present, Jeanna's once cheery and gregarious personality was supplanted by bitterness and pessimism, which devolved into persistent depressed moods she could barely manage. She blamed Dot for many of her struggles, even as an adult.

4- THE ILLNESS STIGMA

Of course, everyone in Rosedale knew the Thornton family seemed clearly predisposed to mental disorders, but their near-fanatical aversion to the stigmas of disease made them soundly repudiate symptoms as a work of Satan, and the victim deemed cursed. Grandma Dora grew up in that climate, in which clearly pathological maladies were deemed a work of the devil that required the sinner to repent of some unknown sin, and receive deliverance. The family honor of a people already afflicted by the past evils of slavery could not be further imperiled by a genetic or biochemical defect, so the culture of demonizing the wounded within their clan prevailed even today. This was why Jeanna's grandmother so deeply feared for her granddaughter. A dread that Jeanna would not only inherit besetting illnesses, but would also suffer the harsh social consequences generations of Thornton women endured for generations often beset Grandma Dora with worry and all she could do was pray.

Jeanna's struggles were not unique; the grandmother grappled with Dot's unnamed symptoms throughout her adolescence. Grandma Dora also acknowledge her own inexplicable crying spells that lasted for hours without cause, as well as the sudden and off-putting switches in her moods. Dot also was both a happy go lucky teen, and an easily provoked time-bomb. Back in Grandma Dora's time, mood disorders were considered a matter of self-control to be managed by the parent. Grandma Dora's mother Luvenia, and all the members of Rosedale Memorial were taught to follow the Bible's prescriptions for rearing their difficult children, or other kin, by using the rod of correction and a firm hand; should neither remedy prevail, the child, parent, and, by extension, the family were determined "cursed by God".

In Rosedale, the fortunes of one's entire family rested largely upon which category the household was assigned. Being accursed relegated an entire people to social and economic ostracism. Families strove by all means to avoid, or evade that classification, even if it meant demonizing their own flesh and blood. The grandmother knew, firsthand what this meant. She was held captive in her grandmother's home after the rape, despite being a victim because her cousin's family wielded social power and he, a scheming predator, could not defame the Thornton clan, so his victim was vilified and the matter buried. These painful recollections drove her fierce protectiveness of her granddaughter and fueled her guilt about ignoring Jeanna's clear signs of distress years ago.

When the woman was six, an old widow in the

neighborhood told Grandma Dora, 'get that girl some spiritual help Dora; that child's been for infected from the womb of her mother'. The sage explained, 'the soul feels everything, including rejection'. 'Somebody didn't want that baby when she was conceived', so Jeanna's soul had been 'fightin' for acceptance all this time, and testing the world to see if she mattered in it'. Grandma Dora considered the theory preposterous - she had been fiercely protective of the grandchild since conception, and believed she urged the child's mother to embrace the baby as a gift from God. She disregarded the fact that her own child was the fruit of rape and was raised largely by her grandmother as she had raised Jeanna. She also failed to realize how Dot too struggled mightily with self-acceptance.

Intuitively, Grandma Dora believed the prophetic words about her grandchild were a metaphor of the Thornton women, and the ache of her own hidden wounds made her consciously reject the truth because she was incapable of coming terms with her own suffering, that unquenchable burning that pleaded for 'belongingness' and love. Each woman she loved had been thwarted in meeting this need, and, over time, they developed such morbid self-hatred, and bitterness that led some, like her great-grandmother to choose death over the inexorable inner suffering. In Jeanna's case, the years of unrequited love, the declined invitations to parties, award ceremonies, and academic honors reinforced her internalized conviction that she was unwanted, and, in some undefined way, irredeemably defective.

When a person arrives at the conclusion that their existence is damnably flawed, what defense can they launch to overthrow crippling hopelessness? The fateful conclusion instigated Jeanna's emotional upheaval. It first started with her increasingly morose disposition, then her inexplicable social withdrawal from her favorite school activities in tenth grade. Grandma Dora asked Jeanna few questions about these changes; she instead watched silently and prayed, consoling herself with Jeanna's continued academic mastery. In hindsight, her silence was collusion, deliberate cooperation with

Jeanna's disease. For more than two years, Jeanna, of course, denied she was troubled, but her grandmother knew the truth would eventually emerge. She discovered Jeanna's suicide notes hidden in one of her diaries while cleaning the bedroom. Despite being the senior class valedictorian, most of her entries spoke of boredom with life, feelings of worthless and implied an as-yet-undetermined plan to die after graduation.

When confronted, Jeanna defensively confirmed the entries, and was taken to Rosedale Health Center, where she was diagnosed with Dysthymia, and a persistent depressive disorder with features much like depression. That she excelled academically but suffered in nearly every other sphere of her social and inner life. While relieved to have a diagnosis, Grandma Dora was incensed that mental illness plagued yet another generation of Thornton women. The ailment was loathsome. Jeanna resented taking anti-depressant medication that made her feel *less like herself*. As time passed and the symptoms persisted, she became increasingly demoralized. Community and church views were often narrow and offered the suffering like her useless antidotes like 'just pray on it', or, '*pray it off*', while assuring full recovery that few, including Jeanna ever realized. Those who possessed '*enough faith*' *and showed* unwavering confidence in such exhortations were crushed when their Dysthymic moods resisted even the most effective treatments.

Treatment for most with the disorder was a mixed bag that included anti-depressants, cognitive behavioral therapy, psychotherapy, family and interpersonal counseling as well as exercise, dietary changes, a stable sleep schedule, as well as no drug or alcohol use. The problem with this regimen, for Jeanna was her increased appetite and weight gain due to hormonal changes. She felt the cure was a bad as the condition, considering its side effects, which included suicidal thoughts and impulses in some cases. Despite her regimen, Jeanna became increasingly discouraged about her nearly twenty years' battle with a diseased that was only moderately abated by her faith, pills, and counseling. It felt like bondage. Jeanna hated being chained to mood-stabilizing drugs and was tired of paying the therapist.

It was Duray' betrayal, and the abortion caused that set her off finally. Jeanna had not taken her anti-depressant medications in more than seven weeks during her unplanned pregnancy to protect the fetus. After the abortion she experienced such a deep and unsearchable sense of despondency that seemed intractable. Transient euphoric emotions about the pregnancy, and her imagined future with Duray lulled Jeanna into a false sense of stability such that, when the depression rebounded with a vengeance, she had no fund of emotional strength and serotonin to withstand the anguish tearing her heart; she viewed the crisis as another disappointment and the fruit of her moral failure.

5- COMING TO UNCERTAIN TERMS

Jeanna's bloated stomach twisted in agony as her mother rose from the chair and stood leaning on the rail while staring into her face. She feigned unconsciousness and Dot gently caressed the restraint on her right wrist and bit her lip to restrain a moan. Her other hand hovered above Jeanna head, gingerly caressing the hair that spread like a wild bush over the hospital pillow. Jeanna listened as Dot prayed in an unknown language, perhaps French. She was beside herself with aversion to her mother's foreign touch; she couldn't shrink from the faint strokes. Impotent rage welled up inside, threatening to explode. 'How dare this stranger dare put her hands on me, the child she abandoned almost twenty years ago!' Jeanna wanted to scream, 'Get the hell off me, you horrible selfish B!@#$, Lord forgive me!' She had never cursed at her mother, or anyone for that matter because she had always been a dutiful Thornton girl who was taught to hate indecorous public behavior.

Let it go.

Oh, heck no! She couldn't shake the bitterness and resentment inside of her heartbroken soul towards her long-absent mother; it had only grown unchecked since childhood. All the years of abandonment and neglect were subsumed beneath Jeanna's academic and professional success, waiting to detonate. If Jeanna wasn't so terrified of Grandma Dora's condemnation, she would have forced her languid tongue to 'cuss her for old and new' with not one hint of remorse. Wrath towards the woman had boiled in her heart for decades, and here she was, touching hair she never combed or plaited.

Jeanna was outraged, but afraid to expose her deception. Her tense body almost shook with hostility as Dot's entreaty was closed with the phrase 'in the name of Jesus'. Jeanna's ears pricked. 'In Whose Name?' Had the sinner found religion in Europe? Dot's conversion seemed inconceivable, and did nothing to improve her standing in Jeanna's eyes. Was her mother, one of the most narcissistic and wanton people she knew, now serving the Lord? Or, was it some pious act? Though burning with curiosity, Jeanna's dread of their unavoidable clash was greater, so she remained unmoving as Dot said, 'Mother wake up; Jeannie's doctor is here'. 'Oh crap, Jeanna thought. 'There is no way I can fool this doctor, but I can't face both of these woman together!' It was bad enough she had to deal with her grandmother now, she also had to come to terms with her past. Worse still, Jeanna had to remain stock-still as Grandma Dora awakened to greet the Asian-looking man who entered the room. His presence was a brief reprieve from scrutiny so she relaxed as her stomach lurched and her bowels churned. Vomit or diarrhea would prevail soon - something had to give, yet the prospect of either reaction occurring outside of a bathroom sickened her more. *'Not yet please, body I need more time!'* She needed to gather enough courage to face the woman she blamed for so much of her anguish, and, make peace with her grief-stricken grandmother.

6-ASSESSMENT & UNDERSTANDING

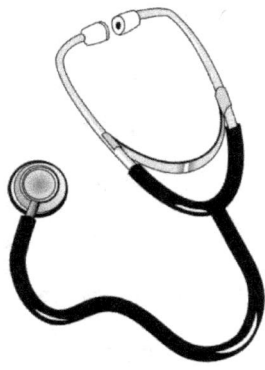

Doctor Sanjeev Muru, the ward's psychiatrist, greeted Dot and the grandmother while turning on a switch that filled the room with searchlight brightness. Terrified that her charade was about to be uncovered, Jeanna's heart raced wildly as she remained motionless despite the excruciating discomfort. *'Damn those %$#@#&^*!#@ Pills! Lord, please forgive me!'* Ironically, Jeanna chose drugs to avoid the agony of other suicide methods; she wanted a smooth transition to eternity, not this humiliating suicide watch at the hospital. Her present tortures seemed a just punishment from God, she guessed. Loopy, philosophical meanderings filled her thoughts, the result of the medicines still coursing through her veins. Though disoriented, Jeanna still felt the weight of the unspeakable indignity and guilt she internalized about her failed attempt and the illness itself.

Here she was, ostensibly successful, beleaguered by inconsolable grief of no clear origin, just plopped mysteriously in her brain. She was 'tired of dealing with this sh—!' (and she did not ask for forgiveness this time- she meant every word, with all of her being). Dr. Muru explained that he was the psychiatrist on call, and explained that he would be monitoring Jeanna's recovery. He inquired about the family medical history and Jeanna, eyes clasped, strained to understand the psychiatrist's broken English and the whispered conversations.

Doctor Muru: (with heavy accent): "Who eez thee mother of these woman? I'd like to ahsk you a few questions about your dawthter. "Does your dawhter av any other family members vat have ever committed or tried to commit suicide?"

Grandma Dora (*Exasperated by Dr. Muru's thick accent,*

she bristled at his query): "First of all Doctor Muroon, is that how you say your name? I'm so sorry, but I can barely understand you! Dotty did you understand what he was saying? How can we learn what's going on with my baby if the doctors don't have a good command of English? Can you come on over here and listen to him again! What did you say again?

Doctor Muru: (*Speaking loudly*) "I zaid does your family av ahny history of mental illness? Has anyone ever made a suicide attempt or completed a suicide?"

Grandma Dora: *(Defensive about family questions and offended by his perceived condescension*): 'First off Doctor Maroon, I am not Deaf or Dumb, I just can't understand you through that thick accent! They can't send us someone else to come in here and ask these questions? And secondly, what does family history have to do with anything? That has nothing to do with my Jeanna! I decree that the Blood of Jesus destroyed all the Thornton curses in our family!'

Doctor Muru: (Confused about her words): 'No, Miss I ahm

not asking about blood diseases; I ahm asking you about mental health disorders ahnd if anyvone in your family ever committed suicide or made attempts?'

Grandma Dora (Exasperated): 'I said the Blood of Jesus Christ heals us! I ain't said anything about any blood disease! I said she was fine until recently, with that preg— Oops! Um, that wasn't supposed to come out! (*Glanced guiltily over at Jeanna's face and Dot's shocked expression*) Lord forgive me, but I'll tell it all if it will help her Doctor! Well, my poor baby got herself knocked up five months ago, just like a lot of us dumb women did, by some no-account thug she called herself in love with, but then she found out he was young enough to be her son, after she had already given him the goods without protection, I guess, since she got herself pregnant. Why would a brilliant woman do that Doctor!? Having unprotected sex at her age! I was shocked Doctor, Maroon (paused).

Grandma Dora: 'Anyway, she accidentally caught the liar with his fiancée' at the Food Lion downtown around three months ago, but she was too embarrassed to make a scene, so she up and got an abortion. I think she was afraid of a public scandal and all, since he was so young; I took her to get it.'

Dot (Surprised and concerned): 'Oh my goodness! She must feel horrible about that! Abortions are terrible! The guilt and shame you feel, even if it's necessary is unbearable! I'm ashamed to admit it but I had one before and I wouldn't wish that pain on anyone, least of all my only child! She always wanted children, even when she was a child!'

Dr. Muru: 'So thee trigger vor these suicide attempt vas thee abortion?'

Grandma Dora: 'Doctor Maroon, I don't know what the trigger was, but I do feel terrible about it because I think the abortion really hurt Jeanna because she's been wanting to get married and to have kids for so long, and she's forty-three, so she is getting too old for babies she feels. I think the straw that broke the camel's back was the fact that she thought he was the One, and she was devastated that he played her for a fool. She had stopped her medications when she got pregnant and the depression must have gotten worse. I think she was mostly ashamed of herself. That no-account fool still had the nerve to be trying to see her! I'm just praying to God that he falls off the face of the earth for deceiving her like that! He was parading around like he was thirty-two with a contractor business, taking her to his mommas' house when the lady was at work! I think she just about paid for all their meals, but she won't tell me. She was lonely; she said working so many hours at the law office does not give you a social life. Doc it's just a mess! You know, I told her he looked too young, but you know these women out here, when they get older. They start to feel so desperate, even when they have so much going for them...'

Doctor Muru: 'Miss, Vat did you mean ven you said thee straw broke thee camel's back?'

Jeanna, who was listening tentatively, absolutely wanted the ground to swallow the entire room, bed and all, so deep was the degradation she felt. 'Grandma, how could you, especially in front of **her**!' As if kinetically in tune with her granddaughter, Grandma Dora's voice trailed off; she realized how intimate the revelations she shared with her estranged daughter and the psychiatrist were. She covered her mouth while staring at Dot, whose stunned expression said it all. The fact that her only child experienced such treachery, and bore the sorrows on her own, without the support of either parent filled Dot with remorse. She wished she had been brave enough to fight for her child when the grandmother assumed custody at her birth.

Back then, Dot was restricted to a peripheral role in her daughter's life growing up. Dot remembered with anger the occasions she tried to assert her authority as Jeanna's mother, and how she was soundly rebuked and made to feel inept and unqualified to parent. Lacking her own sense of belonging, and having been raised by Jeanna's great-grandmother, Luvenia Thornton-Hill most her formative years, Dot surrendered Jeanna completely after the debacle with Jerome. Feelings of failure for having exposed Jeanna to harm convinced her that she was ill-suited to raise her daughter and she gave in to her mother's demands, hopeful that Jeanna would thrive and settle into Rosedale's cliquish community because of her grandmother's social connections.

She stood to face Dr. Muru, who had been listening intently while writing indecipherable notes on the chart. Jeanna's surrogate looked at her quizzically as if to say, 'What are you doing?' Jeanna, meanwhile, remained motionless, as self-recrimination and fever warmed her cheeks. She felt betrayed by her grandmother's sharing of their sworn secret. NO one was to know about the termination. As if reading her granddaughter's mind, Grandma Dora said, 'Oh well, Lord, forgive me, but YOU know my heart!'. She sobbed as tears drenched her ashen cheeks and spattered stains on the red cardigan. Desperation compelled her unbridled sharing of their confidences. As she confessed, heaviness dissipated, so she continued the confessional.

Dot: 'Dr. Muru, I'm sorry I ramble, and I hope she can't hear none of this, but my heart has been so heavy with this for a long time, and now, with my dear husband passed on last year, I have no one to lean on but Jesus. I thought I was gonna lose my mind with worry too! But Doc, I held on to the horns of the altar, like her life depended on it! Yes, I did...but I got tired too, because the disease is so unpredictable! One day, Jeanna would be on her medication, and she would be fine, winning all her cases, and being joyful and productive, coming to church and everything, but then, Bam!"

Dr. Muru: (*looking confused*) 'I'm sowwy, Ma'am, but vat eez thee anchor you are referring to?'

Grandma Dora: "You gotta learn our lingo, Doctor if you want to be helpful! The horns of the altar is PRAYER, ok? But, like I was saying, out of nowhere, Jeanna would crash hard and be unable to get herself out of the dumps. She would say she was fine, but I'd go drop off food or something and the house would be a mess, she'd be stanking in her work clothes, saying she had been too tired to them take off and I'd say, 'All weekend, honey, well, something ain't right about that'. She would say she was fine and brush me off. Then, she stopped coming to church and I told her that church was her anchor and that she would drift far if she didn't keep her coming to service.

Dr. Muru: 'I'm sowwy vat is thee anchor you are talking about? Is that her therapy?'

Grandma Dora: "I'm talking about Jesus Christ, Doctor! She needed to stay connected to God. You probably Hindu or something like that and you don't know nothing about that, but the anchor is the Truth, the Light, the foundation of our Faith is Christ! My baby needed to keep coming to church because she was struggling a lot after she had, you know, that procedure done, and I know she wanted that baby, but the truth is, I was worried how she would even take care of the child since she was so stressed. She's been so hard on herself, Doctor because she really wanted that baby! I think she was delusional enough to think that trifling boy could be man enough to take of the child! Doc it breaks my heart that my Jeanna Rose is so smart and too beautiful to have such low self-esteem, but that's the illness, I guess. I just tried to hold her close because here she is, forty-three now, but she's never had a real man, never been courted and showered with love from the looks of the one or two I seen her run behind, no real kinda loving all her life! She never had good, qualified man, and I think she was lonely. I think she settled for less, you know what I mean? Plus was she into all those toys and sex things she thought she hid from me, but I saw them! Lord have mercy!'

Beside herself with embarrassment, Jeanna wondered how much longer she could keep up her charade as the sickness was worsening. 'Grandma knows about the sex toys? How... I...' She remembered that her grandmother had to retrieve her belongings, and insurance information in the bedroom, would have searched Jeanna's purse, where more than likely, she saw her favored instruments. She always carried one in the small cosmetic case for her especially stressful days at work. Jeanna was grateful she viewed pornography digitally and that her cell-phone was locked. Bemused and resigned to her fate, Jeanna listened quietly and tensely. Grandma Dora was so unpredictable; Jeanna had no idea what else she knew or discovered.

Dr. Muru (Looking confused): 'I'm sowwy? You mean Meez Thornton vas depressed because she have no child, and no anchor, and no altar of horns, and no husband?'

Grandma Dora (Frustrated): Yes, to all of that but mostly it was the illness and she wasn't taking her medication like she should... (pauses and starts to sniffle) ... I told her she was a Queen and when a Queen settles, she loses her Crown of Joy and her Hope... (She paused to wipe her tears before going on).

As Dot sat in the chair weeping silently, Jeanna was disquieted by the proximity; she lay tensely still, pretending to sleep. Hard as she tried, something was thawing in her heart towards Dot and she could find no reason to fight against the bitterness that was dissipating slowly. The doctor prodded: "'Vat else happened bevore the suicide?'

Grandma Dora: 'Well for one thing, Jeanna just started spending and spending all of a sudden these last couple of weeks, like she was stocking up for Armageddon or something. I mean, the stuff was just piling up in all the rooms in her house, and I'd say, 'Chile what is all this?' and she would say 'I just want to bless a few people in my life who have been so good to me over the years' and she was shopping like crazy on that shopping channel and on-line. She sometimes got anxiety in large crowds as a child so she preferred shopping at home.

Dr. Muru (*writing notes, glancing up*): 'So Vere is anxiety disorder in your family?'

Grandma Dora: 'Doctor Maroon, I am not a psychiatrist or psychologist, I just know my baby was scared of large crowds when she was younger and she and got real clingy'.

Dot listened, her eyes fixed on the sleeping form beneath the blue blanket. She hoped her child would never experience the symptoms that plagued her most of her life; the anxiety and excessive fearfulness drove many if not all of her rash decisions, including shacking up with that fiend Jerome. She only overcame them as an adult and through sheer force of the will. Dot felt she had no choice but to survive on her own, away from her mother's rejection and disapprobation, despite the tragic consequences that ensued. She listened desperate to learn all she could about her child's struggles.

Grandma Dora: '…Then she started giving stuff away, even her good bags and her jewelry, so I knew something wasn't right, because Jeanna loves all her junk. She's kind of a hoarder! Lord, that child wouldn't give up nothing, then all of a sudden, she was sharing everything she owned? The police said when they got into her house, it was so jam-packed that there was only a small pathway to walk through!

Dr. Muru: ''So she vas shopping and giving things avay and staying alone?''

Grandma Dora: "That's what I just said! Are you listening to me? I said the clutter was so bad that when the firemen broke in to her house, they could barely walk through the place. They said water came from the bathroom sink upstairs, where by an act of God, that squirrel that Jeanna had been complaining about, fell through with the drop ceiling onto the cold water lever, you know the fancy, one-handled ones? Well, a piece of that ceiling fell on the lever and pushed it forward, which turned on the water and it ran and ran, until it flooded the bathroom, and then, it started running everywhere until it leaked clear through those old wooden floors in that Victorian she owns, and started dripping they say real heavy in the kitchen so her crazy Army guy neighbor came to warn Jeanna, but he couldn't get an answer, so he called 911, and they broke in and found her butt-naked in her bed, Lord have mercy! I thank God for that pest! That squirrel saved Jeanna's life!'

Dr. Muru (looking quizzical): "A squirrel zaved her life? I was not avare that she had a pet... The story is incredible and it is clear from what you zaid vat she showed clear zigns of her intent to harm herself. '

Jeanna strained to eavesdrop, and was transfixed as her grandmother explained how the detested rodent ate through the mesh barriers and snares the pest control agency installed last year, and was apparently nesting just above the bathroom sink when the ceiling gave way. Jeanna of course, knew nothing about her unlikely rescue, and was sure the Rosedale firemen and rescue staff, who loved her grandmother, shared the miraculous happenstance with her and others. Were it not for the pesky squirrel family that nested each year in the walls and attic of Jeanna's Victorian duplex, whose mother squirrel, anxious to build a nest before winter, had not eaten away at the fragile joints suspending the drop ceiling, the barrier would not have given way under the animal's weight that day, falling onto the lever of the modern bathroom faucet, which spouted the water that overflowed onto the bathroom floor, through the floor and subfloor, down to Joel Brown's kitchen and dining room.

Then, if Joel hadn't gone to his landlord, after seeing her car parked in the garage, and knocked on the door for several minutes, he would not have sensed that something was amiss, then called 911, who responded immediately. If the Rosedale police and firemen had not responded quickly, and broken down her door to gain entry, just as she became unresponsive, the suicide attempt would have succeeded. Jeanna's intervention was a miracle that no one would have believed if the frightened squirrel was not seen scampering out of the apartment, and down the stairs by the rescuers who broke down Jeanna's front door. Jeanna vaguely recalled the moments before she lost consciousness, and a cold shiver rushed through her. A flash of recognition struck. In her drunkenness, Jeanna uttered an incoherent, tear-filled rant as she sat on her clutter-filled bed, and filled her mouth twice with the pills, downing them with vodka. Before she lay down with her vibrator, she railed, "God, I know You hate me, but why! What the hell did I do to deserve all this sh— I've been through? I didn't ask to be here! Why all this pain! I've had it! I can't live like this anymore! I can't take another day of this bull--- life! I'm done! You win!"

After a drunken pause, Jeanna downed another swig of vodka, and continued her tirade, saying: 'You made me like this! I'm tired of being sick! I've done all I know to fight this depression! I'm tired! You win! I'm taking these useless pills that never helped anyway, and if they work, I know I'm cursed, and It won't matter anymore God!' The phrase, *'... and if they work, I know I'm cursed'* reverberated in her ears. The overdose should have done it, she knew it! She had calculated the toxic level needed to collapse her systems, and was sure the vodka would accelerate the effect, but, just in the nick of time, that hastily uttered decree demanded Love to answer her desperate cry for help. That despairing exclamation moved God's heart, Jeanna believed.

Through the most unlikely intervention, God answered a desperately suicidal woman's plea. The revelation was humbling. To think that even in her most debauched state, God sought the rescue of His communion with her reprobate, broken soul? God, in His Loving wisdom accepted all petitions including Jeanna's apologetic, expletive-filled rants. In that pivotal moment, when all her strength was sapped, God listened and, answered in a way that was so unlikely, so far-fetched, that all everyone could say was, 'That had to be God'. The miracle was far above her Harvard degree understanding. The revelation was humbling; she had never felt more unworthy than she did at that moment. The knowledge was simply too wonderfully kind for a person who rejected even self-compassion. God's love is never too far from the cries of anyone who dared to call upon the Name of the Lord. Jeanna never imagined a Love firmly in touch with all of her infirmities. A glimmer of new Joy crept in even as tears fell liberally. For the first in a LONG time, Jeanna was overshadowed by LOVE and her soul knew it. She silently thanked God for the rodent and her family.

In that heartening moment, sudden, sharp and stabbing pains convulsed Jeanna's abdomen. She needed to vomit, but God help her, she still wasn't prepared for the look in her mother's eyes, or to face the solicitous stares of her loved ones. She was still broken, but not ashamed. Tightening her fists as the rumblings increased, she moaned inwardly as Grandma Dora continued her longwinded confessional, grieved that her closest ally freely shared such intimate details with Dot present. Dr. Muru, clearly in a rush to see other patients, said he still needed to complete psychosocial assessment of the Thornton family. 'I veally need to go Meez Thornton, so I just ave to ahsk a few more questions about your dawther'.

Oblivious to his request, Dot's mother continued, relieved to purge her soul by sharing more than necessary about Jeanna's struggles, while avoiding direct questions about the family predilections. She volunteered that Jeanna thought her parents hated her (Dot winced when she heard it, much to the grandmother's delight), and told Dr. Muru, 'the poor girl always wondered why she was the only Thornton with dark skin and her mother's grey eyes'. 'At times', she added, 'Jeanna even wondered if she belonged in the family, because so many of her relatives, who were light bright and almost white treated her with such meanness when they were growing up'.

It was true. The color discrimination she experienced within her own family was severe; Jeanna stopped herself from unconsciously nodding in agreement. She recalled feeling like an outcast, and staying to herself during family events to cope with her kin's rejection. As she reminisced, Dot resumed sitting near her bed, and stared blankly at the leather wrist restraint confining Jeanna's right arm. Suddenly, she jumped up and, ignoring her mother's glare, approached the doctor. She was about to speak when her mother hissed, "Dotty I'm sorry, but I blame you and that sorry a--, Lord forgive me, no-account loser for most of Jeanna's issues! You know, that drunk fool had the nerve to show up here trying to see a child he hasn't seen in decades! I was flabbergasted! The nerve! The deacon asked him to leave, and I told him to send her past due child support!'

Angrily, Dot blurted, 'How could you! You know he tried for years to have a relationship with his only child, but you, with your greedy self, blocked him every time, threatening him with harassment and spreading lies in the church, until they drove him away too! What kind of Christian woman does that?' The mother and daughter's eyes locked for what seemed like an eternity and Dr. Muru, uncomfortable with the exchange, cleared his throat to get their attention, and told them he needed to check Jeanna's vital signs.

'What! My daddy came to see me?' A child-like giddiness rose up in her. Jeanna always yearned to know the man she favored. As Dr. Muru approached, Jeanna went as limp as she could, and tried to slow her racing heart. Dr. Muru leaned close to the patient, listened to her racing heart as she lay immobile in the bed, and said something about her slight fever. He mumbled absently that Jeanna should be awake. 'Yikes, I'm done' Jeanna guessed but then, the doctor glanced between the two combatting parents, and said "I ave summoned a nurse's aide to change the patient's soiled diaper'. Dot gasped in dismay while Grandmother Dora said, 'Lord have mercy; the child has loss control of her bowels!' moaning as the tears fell afresh. Jeanna felt slightly relieved and sighed

"Oh Well it was puke or poop, something had to give".'

Jeanna restrained her bowels as long as she could, but the diarrhea prevailed. She remained silent despite being perplexed and angry about her grandmother's sabotage of the connection she desperately longed to have with her mother and father. For years, Jeanna attributed their absences largely to neglect. 'How could you be so selfish grandma?! I cried for them every day and you did nothing to assure me that they gave a damn, Lord forgive me!' She raged within, and reclined lifelessly while the aides loosened her restraints and rolled her gently on her side to remove the padding beneath her.

All of the humiliation of the past months could not match being rolled over like a heavy slab of meat, then bathed like an invalid by complete strangers under the watch of her mother and grandmother who observed the ministrations with wagging heads. Dr. Muru excused himself briefly and exited the room.

7-FACING THE PAST

Dot complained to no one in particular, 'I see no reason for an unconscious patient to be held hostage in those dreadful restraints. Can the doctor reassess my child and get them removed?' Jeanna's grandmother replied, 'You have some nerve talking about "my child"-she hasn't been YOUR child in years!' Her daughter was unmoved by the reproach and whispered haughtily, 'You know Mom, you can't indict me about my child without convicting yourself and this whole dysfunctional family! You KNOW how YOU fought me tooth and nail to destroy my relationship with my daughter the same way Grandmother did with you! But I'm here now, and I won't be intimidated anymore'. You will not keep me away from my child! You can't lie and use Jeanna against me anymore to make up for your own absentee parenting Mother!'

Grandma Dora was stunned and infuriated. 'How dare you say those things to me you little – Lord help me!' Just then, Dr. Muru entered the room, keenly aware of the tension filling the air. 'Um, Misses, I need to finish thee assessment please.' Jeanna, confused, and disappointed, remained unmoving, her foggy mind reeling. Did Grandma Dora really conspire to sever the ties she desperately needed with her mother and father? Did she know how traitorous that would feel if it was true? All the memories of feeling discarded like trash rushed forward like fire in her throat, but the scream could not be released. Unsated rage pulsed through her veins, causing her left leg to involuntarily shake. She squeezed her buttocks, tensing her body to still her jerking limb, which neither adversary detected as they clashed.

Still nonplussed and concerned Jeanna might awaken during their hostile exchanges, the grandmother waved her hand dismissively towards Dot while pacing the floor chanting, 'Lord Jesus, help me because I wanna hurt this grown snooty heifer so bad, so bad, Lord help me, but the Spirit won't let do it! Help me Lord, please, to make peace with the workers of iniquity, Lord, please!' Dot, annoyed by her mother's histrionics, followed dramatic suit and prayed "Lord Jesus, I know YOU want the truth to be known so we can all be set free, so please break up that lying spirit in the room, and make my tongue plain and clear, Lord, please! Amen!'

Jeanna, with great effort, quashed the amused laughter threatening to expose her act. Not to be outdone by her daughter, Grandma Dora reared back, ready to burst into song when Dr. Muru exclaimed, "Misses please! Deez behaviors are not gud for thee patient and she vill avaken soon enough and she vill be need you both, so please, please let us complete your family assessment, yes? Now I need to ahsk, are there any other family with a history of mental illness?' Grandma Dora pretended to ignore the question, and began murmuring, 'Lord help me to hold out' as she paced the quarters. Dot ignored this evasion and shared their story.

Dot: "Doctor Maroon, yes, there is a LOOONNNNG history of mental illness in this family Doctor. Thornton men too, but especially our women. My mother has had anxiety issues since she had me at fifteen. They said she had a mental breakdown after she had me, I'm not sure, I just know I was raised by Grandma Luvenia since I was three months old, then my mom came and tried to take me when I got pregnant with my child, but I was grown by then.' I know my grandmother said my mother has really bad mood swings, and they were afraid she would hurt me, so ---'

Grandma Dora (Interjecting): 'How dare you put all my business on the street! My business has nothing to do with my grandchild Doctor Maroon! I was raped by my first cousin just like my great-great grandmother was, yet everybody blamed me! I was just thirteen and yes, I was a kid, and I had a real hard time with how the church and everybody treated me, so I did lose it for a while, when my mother took over, but we lived in the same house until Dot got older so my mom put me out so that she could…" Painful realization made her silent; she recognized the pattern. Thornton girls were abandoned or orphaned by their birth mothers and fathers for generations! She had committed the trespass as well. Bowing her head, she resignedly sat in the chair, tears running, and motioned for her daughter to continue. 'Keep going, it needs to come out'.

Jeanna, in sync with her grandmother, averted her face slightly as tears fell. She had no idea her grandmother had been raped, and that there was a pattern of sexual exploitation of the women in the family, which no one discussed. It almost persisted with Jeanna, if her mother had not returned from the shopping trip. Dot looked compassionately at her mother then continued: "Dr. Muru, I never shared this with anyone, but I was diagnosed with Past-Traumatic Stress Disorder five years ago in France and I was getting treatment and counseling until I came here. After my child was taken away from me, I was angry and hurt, so I rebelled a lot, ran the streets, and I looked for my father, who I've been told is a distant cousin, and I tried all kinds of ways to find myself, then I used people, mostly to try to get out of Rosedale. The memories were so painful here! Do you know what it's like to feel lost? That's how I felt all the time. Sometimes I was promiscuous just to keep a sponsor, and I did a lot of things I am too ashamed to even mention. These folks here are so cruel and judgmental, like they don't have skeletons, always whispering about me at church, and I got tired of it'

The words deeply resonated with Jeanna; she felt kindred to the experiences her mother detailed, and even more troubled about facing her sworn adversary. 'What do I say to them', she debated, longing to break her silence, if her still-swollen tongue would cooperate. The muscle felt leaden as she silently rolled it over her teeth. 'What will they say to me?' The unknown terrified her.

Dr. Muru (Uncomfortable with the unsolicited narrative): 'Misses, I think I ave enough information here so vee can continue with the evaluation...'

Grandma Dora (interrupting): Dotty, I knew something was off, but I had no idea! You would be mad and raging one minute, nice another and crying. I was scared for the baby...

Dot: 'Mother, I could never hurt my daughter! You never gave me a chance! You wanted her for yourself it seemed! I was so angry, I tried to leave with Nathaniel, but his family blocked us and sent him off to Atlanta. I thought you were in on that too, and we both hated you. Nathaniel and I were in Love momma! We were so in love, and you forced him to stay away by threatening to file rape charges against him, and the family hated you for that, so they stayed away too. He wanted to marry me and he was my first love! We were just church kids trying to find our way, but everyone sabotaged our love. Y'all don't know how you devastated us. He was kind, and good, and he never put his hands on me, like all the other men. I don't think I ever got over him. I never had a chance.'

Grandma Dora (Feeling guilt and remorse): "Honey I am so sorry! I was trying to protect you and my grandbaby from the hardships I went through, and I was so scared someone would touch on that baby girl like I caught that old disgusting neighbor trying to molest you when you were just a baby... we tried to kill him and drove him out of town...'

Dot: Mother I knew what you were trying to do - you just went about it the wrong way, and we all suffered. Then, I choose Jerome to get away from you, and I can't explain it Momma, but he had a power over me! I was so desperate for my daddy and love; I felt as if a Jerome gave them both to me, but it was twisted abusive love. The only thing that saved me was counseling I started secretly and going back to church. They have wonderful choirs over there and they appreciate "our kind of music", Momma. Getting back to God gave me the courage to finally leave Jerome; he treated me more like his child-slave than a lover. It took me years of sexual, emotional, and financial abuse to get

tired of him and the things I let him do to me were appalling. I still have flashbacks sometimes, but not that often. Since I returned to Christ, and forgave Jerome for his abuse, I cope better. Forgiveness helps. I especially had to forgive myself for days when I struggle, and for the years I let that evil man steal from me. When Jeanna is ready, I'm going to share this with her and I hope she will find it in her heart to forgive me. '

Jeanna shivered as she recalled her own abusive episodes with another loser she chose; a selfish boar who used to grab her arm, or move her forcefully when they were in pubic, as if to regulate her movement, like she was his child. Richard's "micro-aggressions", she learned from her therapist, were a form of control and manipulation meant to "keep her in her place", like he said one day, and for six months, he succeeded, until she caught him "regulating" another woman in town. Yes, Jeanna thought, God does show us where to look, as long as we are willing to see. Their stories seemed to mirror similar heartbreak, and compassion for her once-hated parent was awakened. Nonetheless, Jeanna remained guarded, afraid, and still slightly disoriented.

Grandma Dora (crying) Chile, he put his hands on you?

Why did you stay? You've always been able to come back home! I hoped what I went through would never happen to my child (still crying)'

Dot: To what Momma? The same kind of control and verbal abuse? No freedom to raise my child, and you treating me like I'm crazy? I couldn't let my daughter see you treat me like that, and the truth is, I hated it here! The people are terribly racist in Rosedale, especially the light folks! I hated the whole color issue, and I felt guilty about my privileges here over other folks, even my child. I was afraid to fail her and afraid of my own shadow. I'm hoping to stay here until Jeanna gets better, but as soon as my baby heals, she's gonna need a fresh start, especially if, knowing her, anyone else got letters like mine! She can be quite vindictive!'

Grandma Dora: 'She is not going anywhere! This is the only home she has ever known.'

Jeanna listened, and rejoined wordlessly, "Actually I feel stifled in this town; I never liked living here. My worst experiences are here, Grandma.' Of course, no one heard her. Fatigue, or medicine enveloped her like a warm blanket and Jeanna dozed off, while both of her parents negotiated Grandma Dora's resistance to change.

Dot: "She is forty-three, Mother, and if she decides to go to the moon, that's her business! You can't keep trying to control people- it's driven by fear my counselor said."

Dr. Muru (visibly frustrated): Thank you both vor your time. I'm going to check Miss Thornton one more time before I do my wounds (moved toward the patient, shaking his head)'. Jeanna's mothers were oblivious to anything but the enormity of the revelations shared.

"I surely don't want Jeanna to be so desperate for love, as I was. I let Jerome control and manipulate me until my self-esteem hit rock bottom" Dot explained. "You know, can lose your mind over someone momma! I swear I was nearly gone, until I received my daughter's letter; I knew it was a cry for help! Something got a hold of me that day... I left everything, my social life, all the connections, everything He controlled, everything He infected" Dot's tears flowed profusely now, and she waited regain her composure. Her daughter also listened and cried soundlessly. Years of hurt seemed purged with each droplet, and Jeanna let the healing flow wash over her soul. She realized how isolated both of them, mother and grandmother, must have felt trying to bear the weight of generations of Thornton women on their lonely shoulders. Her daily battles felt quite similar to their journey.

Dot: (Wiping her eyes, continued): Mom, I took my diamonds, all the things I could sell, and the money I stashed after I begged him like a child for an allowance all those years. He would ask me for a full accounting of every dime and treated me like I couldn't be trusted, when he was the deceiver and charlatan. He told me I would never have the guts to leave everything he gave me, which was worthless compared to my dignity! That's when I turned to God. I was desperate! He is a truly a Wonderful Counselor Who showed me how to get my documents Jerome hid from me! Do you know God will show you where to look! When I was ready, so was He.'

Grandma Dora (inspired, but defensive): 'Yes, God is able

to make all things possible and new Chile. I just want Jeanna to get the help she needs, and I don't want you here if you're not sticking around to support her and me.

Dr. Muru (returned): "Misses, I ahm ready to do assessment, I vill return these afternoons vhen your dawhter is avake to check on her ahnd to finish, ok?'

They remained oblivious to the physician, and never heard the door click, or the lighting dim as he departed the room.

Grandma Dora: 'I just don't understand why you left us the way you did. You are my only child and I was so hurt when you left suddenly. I want to know what I did wrong Dotty.'

Dot: 'Do you know what it is to be trapped Mother? To be afraid of the fragile security you put in the hands of another human being because you neither loved nor trusted yourself? I do. I did just that for more than eighteen years... (paused, held back tears). I was the child of a child with a child with no idea about what to do for my daughter and you made me feel like couldn't care for me or my child. Momma, I stayed away because I was ashamed! I am so sorry I left you. So much was wrong with me, I was out of my own control, and I knew my child deserved a better mother, like you said after that incident with Jerome. I gave her up.' Dot burst into muffled crying; her mother shushed her for fear that Jeanna would awaken to hear the sordid family revelations. Dot fearing the same, excused herself and rushed to the bathroom.

Jeanna awakened briefly as the bathroom door clicked, and was about to doze again; her grandmother gazed at her charge from the corner where she and Dot were beginning to come to terms with the family story. Sordid and devastating as it was, they were still here, stillt standing, and, by the grace of God, she believed, they were all together as it should be. 'Lord I don't know how You're going to fix this mess, but if you can save my grandbaby with a nasty squirrel, You can do anything and more. I just ask You for the wisdom to come to terms with this family affliction, so that we can help Jeanna overcome her struggle Lord....'

Just then, her own daughter exited the bathroom and asked, glancing at Jeanna, 'Really, Mom, what is the prognosis for my daughter?' Grandma Dora snorted contemptuously after that statement, but knew she had to relinquish control by sharing the fear about Jeanna's recovery. 'Mother, will she be the same brilliant lawyer as before when she awakens? I'm concerned'. Grandma Dora echoed the same lament as she whispered, 'Dotty all we can do is pray. It's all in His hands and we just have to trust

God and wait. She's still sleeping so let's get something from the cafeteria and get back here before Dr. Maroon

returns.' Dot chuckled, 'Mother, I think his name is Muru, not the color Maroon!' The elder retorted, 'Muru, Maroon, it's all the same to me!' and laughed inaudibly as the door clicked, awakening Jeanna.

8-THE GOOD, BAD, UGLY THUTH

Jolted and sensing she was alone in the bedroom, she stirred from her slumber drowsily. Tentatively, Jeanna opened eyes, afraid, pleading, 'Lord, please get me out of this mess! Please heal my eyes, please!' Slowly, she lifted her lids and was relieved that, after several blinks, her vision came into singular focus. 'Thank God!' she thought gratefully. Nausea was ever-present, but abated by Jeanna's half-fetal sleeping position and her controlled breathing. Vomiting would be a sure giveaway that she was alert, and despite all the Kumbaya moments between Dot and her grandmother, Jeanna still struggled with such deep-rooted hostility towards her birth mother and doubted she could allow the vulnerability of forgiveness to break the chains of guardedness she forged all these years. Ambivalence twisted her heart. She knew she would have to face her sworn nemesis, just not now, not in this wretched state. Rolling her tongue, she felt the edge of her molars and rejoiced that sensation was returning. The door opened slowly and she guessed Dot and her grandmother returned so she affected slumber, repositioning her arms

Instead of hushed conversation, there was complete silence. Her heart beat quickly; she questioned who entered the room so stealthily. Was it one of her victims, whom she'd destroyed with the swoop of her pen? Was it Duray, whose attempt to see her days ago was obstructed by her grandmother? Despite trepidation, a calm entered her heart as she remained unmoving. A lone visitor approached her bed. He spoke with deep-voiced sadness, uttering her name repeatedly, as he stood at her bedside.

Nathaniel: 'Jeanna, Jeanna, Jeanna, I'm so sorry daughter!

Please don't die, not like this! I need to make this right and I need you to pull through! I know you can't hear me but I know your spirit is alert and hears everything daughter. I want you to know I tried to be here for you, to become a good father, but I was afraid of going to prison for a crime I did not willfully commit against your mother! We loved each other, and I was intending to marry her one day after I made something of myself, so I stayed away and got my education, and worked to build a life for you and your mother. When I came to get you, your grandmother said Dot ran off with another man, and she had custody.

Nathaniel paused, fighting his own tears and anger and continued: "Your grandmother told me no court of law in Georgia was going to give a child to a rapist, and warned me and my family to stay away. The church demonized me badly, and I was so heartbroken over your mother that I gave up and starting drinking. I was depressed, that I lost my daughter and my future wife. But, I never gave up hope. When the local news talked about your suicide attempt, I came immediately! You were right under my nose! I'll make it all up to you, I promise!

"Daddy!" Jeanna had never seen Nathaniel face to face; while she knew she possessed many of his features, including his ebony tone, she had no idea what those traits were. She fought to hold back tears as he continued talking. His voice was strong, comforting and assuring, a soothing baritone that made her feel safe, despite her bonds. He smelled of a rich scent, and spoke with a fervent, but polished eloquence. She knew he went to Morehouse, and the story ended from there. It was as if Nathaniel had fallen off the face of the earth, leaving a gaping void of questions and anger. 'Why did you give up so quickly Father?' While his elucidation shed light on his absence Jeanna was disappointed at his cowardice and his family's neglect of an innocent grandchild.

As if sensing her questions, Nathaniel added, 'We all failed you Jeanna, but you don't know how powerful your family was in this town, how by one word of your Great-uncles and Miss Luvenia, people would be run out of town, ostracized in church and social life, and how cruel the gossip was about us. If I hadn't left, my parent's feared the church vigilante's and the Thornton's would have destroyed me. You were just a baby, and you may not know this, but your family helped found this community most people submitted to them out of fear and because they had real power. My parents couldn't open up their dry-cleaning and grocery stores without paying their respects to the clans in Rosedale, and your family happened to be the biggest at that time. Nothing moved without their approval. When things happened between me and your momma, they saw to it that my parent's businesses suffered, and my parents relocated near Atlanta, then back to Chicago and they never came back. You have no idea what the Thornton's did to us over a lie. We were in love, and your jealous grandmother and her crazy kin broke us up.'

That truth about Jeanna's crazy family struck her. She was astounded how a few cruel words could wreak havoc that endured for decades in families. Resentment rose and subsided. Her grandmother and her kin wronged her all these years, but she had to let it go. After all, her father was right here.

The father continued: 'It took me and my family years to recover from the hell we went through, and I still never gave up. You have family waiting on you in Chicago, and my mother has forgiven your horrible grandmother because moving was the best thing we could have done! Our businesses flourished in Atlanta and Chicago and I have expanded them. Don't you worry daughter, you can start fresh—'

Just then, Dot and her mother entered; Dot dropped her cafeteria tray, and its contents flew helter-skelter. 'Oh my God, Nathaniel, how did you get in here? What are you doing?' Jeanna's grandmother asked, 'What the hell are you doing back in her room? I thought we told you—'

Nathaniel interrupted stating, 'You can't ever again stop me from seeing my only child Miss Dora! Your Thornton power over me and my family is over! I only left the other day to avoid a confrontation, since the press and newspaper were here, camping out, talking about some squirrel saved Jeanna's life when it fell through the drop ceiling, and accidentally turned on her water, making it overflow? Is that true?' Mortification drained all the ecstasy of Nathaniel's presence from Jeanna's heart, as she realized the extent of unwanted notoriety. The local press knew she attempted to kill herself? That meant EVERYONE, including her exes and victims would soon come 'a-hollering' seeking compensation possibly for damages, and God knows what else.

Grandma Dora (Angrily):'We don't want or need you here Nathaniel, and if I have to call security, I will, so please leave quietly'.

Not everyone shared that sentiment. Dot was bent over near the exit, nervously and excitedly remembering her first love. She discreetly checked her appearance while cleaning up the cafeteria spill, sizing up quickly the man she never stopped loving. He was now about 6'3", slender but muscular, with a narrow waist and long legs. He smelled delightful of a familiar musk. 'Is that Creed? That cost at least $200. I believe Jerome wore that scent.' She remarked at his polished shoes, crepe wool trousers, the viscose and cotton shirt she too would have paired with the Hound's-tooth jacket and admired his confident bearing. Confidence was so sexy on a man, especially one she admittedly still loved. Dot's reverie was interrupted by Nathaniel's curt retort to her mother.

Nathaniel: 'Miss Dora, you should know that I am the Vice-chairman of the Board at this institution, and I can surely come and go as I please to assess patient care, especially as it pertains to my only child. You should know I only left the other day so that I could direct the press to stop hounding Rosedale staff; I squashed the sensational story about the squirrel. I'm Jeanna's father, and I will do whatever I need to do to ensure her best interests are reserved. I will not be leaving her side. Now, if you wish, we can do this amicably, or you can be asked to leave if you dare to sabotage my tie to my only child again. Are we on the same page Miss Thornton?'

Despite having unflinching loyalty to her grandmother, Jeanna's heart leaped for joy as she heard these affirming words from the father she longed for all her life. 'God thank You for bringing my parents back to me.' Her dad's presence was God's answer to childhood prayers Jeanna abandoned long ago.   Remembering her father's words, she wondered if, after all these years, her parents might reclaim a long-lost love. Could it never be too late to dream about love? If they could, shouldn't she reclaim so hope? Jeanna soberly questioned, 'If I had died, would my parents have found one another?'

9- FINDING WORDS, HEALING SCARS

"Other people are going to find healing in your wounds. Your greatest life messages and your most effective ministry will come out of your deepest hurts.

— Rick Warren

Jeanna's grandmother was incensed; she trembled with anger and countered, 'I don't give a damn, Lord forgive me, who you are in this hospital! You have some nerve coming here after all these years, with your expensive clothes, and the same arrogance you had years ago, you and your high-falutin family! You all came to our town like you were gonna take over years ago, and I wasn't letting you have your way with my only child! What do you want from us!' Dot was shocked at her mother's unveiled jealousy of the Jones family, and her inveterate bitterness towards Nathaniel, who was only a kid himself when they courted. "Momma what's wrong with you! Nathaniel came from a good family, and they did nothing, absolutely NOTHING to you. Where is all that anger coming from?

Jeanna lay stunned. Venomous jealousy and envy oozed like pus out of Grandma Dora's words. Why was she so unreasonably jealous of the Jones family, whose only transgression was their son falling in love with Jeanna's mother? Her animus made no sense, and piqued Jeanna's concern. What else was her grandmother hiding? Nathaniel offered a vague justification that seemed too incredible to imagine. Nathaniel paused. then breathed deeply and added: 'Miss Dora, I had nothing to do with whatever happened back in the day between my parents and you, but I know my mother was innocent, and deserved none of the injuries you inflicted. The Bible says that jealousy is as cruel as the grave, and I guess that's true for you Miss Dora. My momma forgave you and moved on, but I haven't forgotten. I forgave you too, so unless you want to wake up laying dogs...'Grandma Dora stared with fear in her eyes, as Nathaniel's words registered with her conscience. She felt hamstrung by his knowledge, which bruised her pride. He looked just like the senior Nathaniel, except taller.

Their liaison was an unexpected comfort during an abusive period in her marriage. It was completely unintentional, as Mr. Jones was a chivalrous and generous leader in their community. It happened naturally, over time when one spends inordinately long periods of time in the Missions department, where outreach projects were common during the upheavals of the Civil Rights Movement. Nathaniel adored his wife, Constance, though she was a retiring hypochondriac afflicted with seemingly chronic ailments. He came to care deeply for Dora and her plight at home. She was also firmly attached to Lewis, who despite his unpredictable drunken rages, was a devoted provider and faithfully attended church. The family lacked nothing, but violent outbursts over petty insults or Dora's perceived "disrespect" were common. The Thornton men intervened after one particularly harrowing incident. When Lewis threatened to kill Dora if she left him. It was during the imposed separation between them that Dora fell in love with Jeanna's paternal grandfather. They both knew it was illicit and futile, as neither intended to end their marital ties, but neither could deny the passion burning between them, which they never consummated. The nearest intimacy was that long embrace in the church basement after they prayed for the grace to end their soul tie.

As they disentangled and kissed gently, the son bounded down the basement stairs to advise his father that mother was not well. He saw the pair as they released their lip hold. 'Dad, what are you doing with Dotty's mother!' They stood startled. His father calmly answered, 'Son it's not what it looks like, I was just praying for Mrs.

White.' Nathaniel countered, "That's not what it looks like at all father, and I'm telling Mama!' He ran up the stairs, his father trailing after him. The senior turned briefly as he climbed the stairs and said, 'I love you Dora, I really do, but you know this cannot be'. Dora, with tear-filled eyes, agreed, 'Yes Nate, I know...I love you too!' She sat forlornly in the cafeteria chair, sobbing brokenheartedly as Nathaniel wiped a falling droplet from his cheek and left her alone and disconsolate.

The elder Jones was able to convince his son not to further impair his mother's poor health with false accusations that would tear their family apart. "Son, you know I adore your mother and always have, but sometimes, adults make mistakes, and all we can do is pray, move on, and never let them happen again, do you understand what I am saying son? I'm depending on you to help your mother by not sharing this with her - I assure you that nothing happened between me and Mrs. Thornton-White". The matter was never discussed again, but the incident left Nathaniel mistrustful of Dotty's mother. When she became pregnant with Jeanna years later, Dora, still pining after the elder Jones, feared a family tie would be too combustible and fought against the love-struck teens for her own emotional protection. Both were unwitting casualties of her unrequited love for Nathaniel Jones, Sr.

Jeanna was equally unsettled by the exchange and also quite hungry. The intravenous food only provided calories and nourishment for comatose patients; she was fairly alert and certainly conscious. The rumblings were either impending vomiting or more diarrhea, and her discomfiture was stifling. Burning to explore her father's issue with Grandma Dora, trepidation constrained her. It was emotionally overwhelming to be in recovery with parents she hadn't seen in decades, and to hear first-hand the role the Thornton's played in their absence. Of utter importance was understanding the relationship Dot once shared with Nathaniel Jones, Jr. How was she feeling, seeing him after all this time? Questions crept in: 'Could they reunite?' but Grandma Dora disrupted this daydream with her nasty reply to Nathaniel.

There would be no more secrets in this family, at least between the grandmother and her children. Besides, the grandmother felt there was nothing illicit about her love for Nathaniel's father. "Listen young man, I'm too old to be held hostage by anyone! God knows I repented for getting close to your father years ago, and we would have remained friends were it not for the untimely sins of his son and my daughter! Your father and I NEVER had an affair, let me tell you that! He loved your mother so much he would never do anything to damage their marriage, or mine for that matter" Nathaniel glanced at Jeanna, then Dot and nodded with understanding. The elder Nathaniel cherished his wife, and was her primary caretaker until her untimely death two years ago. He knew his father suffered many years in their imperfect marriage, but never complained.

"I know Mrs. Thornton" Nathaniel assented. "Grandma Dora continued, saying, "We were both having problems, and we became friends, real friends who loved each other purely. We never had sex, if that's what you thought young man! No, our love was simple, and honest, and a gift from God. I might've been hasty in worrying about you and Dot's situation, and thinking it would be too awkward, but the real truth is, I was hurt that my child was repeating the same sad family story, getting knocked up at a young age out of wedlock. I did not think she was some hot-behind sneaking around in church closets, so I blamed you because you were older, and you should know better.' Dot blushed with embarrassment and exclaimed "Mother!"

Her plea went ignored by her mother, who added, "I also thought you were gonna take her away when I was just getting reconnected to her. I was a teen mom, and my mother raised Dot most of her life, so she knows what Jeanna went through all these years. My bark is bigger than my bite; I regret that we Thornton's victimized your parents in any way. I don't want my grandbaby hurt, and I don't want my starry-eyed looking child to be still looking at you like you are the same crush she had when she was fourteen." Flushed with embarrassment, Dot retorted, "Mother this is not about me! You are not about to do that evasive, bait and switch on me to avoid questions! So you

Had a crush on me would-be-father-in-law? I thought something was fishy about how you two looked at each other when I was a kid!' Nathaniel interposed, 'Truthfully none of that matters anymore. Our Jeanna is still recovering, and there is a lot more to be discussed to move her forward with her illness. I looked at her charts; she was diagnosed more than fifteen years ago with Dysthymia...' Grandma Dora, offended by his officiousness, asked 'Um, excuse me Mr. Jones, but I've been handling her health care needs for all those years you just mentioned, so we don't need another Dr. Maroon talk, we need to pray she wakes up, and that we can move her forward. I had no idea the press were here! Well, she is pretty accomplished here in Rosedale, so...'

Just then, Dr. Muru returned with nursing staff to do bloodwork and check on Jeanna was so disarmed by the provocative disclosures that the doctor's arrival unnerved her. 'Oh my God, how am I going to pull this off? It's been such an emotional upheaval, listening to all their stories! I'm sure my ruse is up!' She laid there, heart racing, determined to stall her encounter, but fearful the illness would no longer cooperate with her plan.

10 -EMBRACING CHANGE

Accompanied by a resident and nurse, the psychiatrist pulled out his examining pen to look in Jeanna's eyes and leaned over to open her lids. She felt Dr. Muru, with labored breath, lean forward. He reeked of curry and unfortunately, sweat. It was more than she could bear. Suddenly, she lurched forward as a projectile of bile launched from her stomach onto the stethoscope and jacket of the sheepish resident standing at the end of her bed. The resident calmly backed up and excused herself. Coughing uncontrollably, Jeanna wretched, as a colorful array of vomitus filled the bowl now in front of her. The display ended with dry heaving and Dot, who had an especially powerful aversion to human waste, especially puke, sat away from the scene feeling dizzy.

'I'm so sorry everyone, I literally get ill when I see or smell— (pointing towards daughter, holding nose)'

'You mean vomit, Dotty?' Smiling, but very concerned for his daughter, Nathaniel watched Jeanna's mother as she covered her mouth and raced to the lavatory. Dora glanced between the two and grinned briefly while holding her grandchild's hand. 'It's still there, Dotty' he thought. The butterflies, the excitement remained steadfast after all these years, he realized. First love feelings he cherished from the first time he met the petite, loud church girl at Youth Choir practice years ago seemed refreshed the moment he saw her, as flawless as he always remembered. The Valentino shoes, her Chanel bag, and the Burberry dress fit her petite. but voluptuous frame perfectly.

Dotty, as he called her, was still a paragon of fashion, her grey-flecked hair pulled into a neat bun, pale skin as smooth as he remembered it. She was fifty-eight looking less than forty, and Nathaniel longed to express his immutable love. 'Yes, she's still single Nathaniel'

Grandma Dora whispered, thinking, 'Oh well, at least they can have a chance at real love.' Nathaniel passed a grateful glance at Dotty's mother, wanting to say his father was a widower, like her, but he remained silent. His focus was on his long-lost, desperately awaited family. They had been irreplaceable all these years. He still wanted his first love.

Freed from the restraints by Dr. Muru after she was interviewed, and deemed lucid enough to sign a no harm contract, Jeanna was groggy, in pain, but happy. Dr. Muru informed the family that a suicide hold would remain in effect for seventy-two hours, and a reassessment would be performed at that time. Crestfallen that she would remain under the hospital's watch despite the agreement, Jeanna nonetheless was grateful that, for once in a long time, she was happy to be alive. Perhaps it was the serotonin levels increased by the anti-depressant medication, the culmination of the day's events, her reunification with her parents, or, most importantly, the miraculous intervention of the squirrel.

All Jeanna knew was that she was overjoyed with hope again. She felt loved in a way she had never experienced before. She knew God loved her for real, especially with the unlikely intervention facilitated by that hated vermin. She lisped a fervent, 'Thank you God!' through her still slightly impaired tongue. Miraculously, unlike some patients on ventilators, there was no long-term damage to her larynx or speech. Jeanna would make a full recovery Dr. Muru stated, but she would need to accept her illness with grace, while following the prescribed regimen needed to manage it successfully.

Jeanna feared the loss of speech, and the demise of a career she may likely need to resume in another town; she mailed a tendered resignation last week. Oh, the caprice, and impulsivity of emotions! Jeanna was chagrined – there was so much she to deal with, including the fallout from her rash decisions, but Jeanna reached for compassion instead of indicting herself. The pathology of mental disorders in the Thornton family, she realized, was no longer her burden. Generations of women in her clan had fought valiantly while others surrendered. The odds were clearly in her favor; God saved her life! Standing with her mother in recovery and freed from the scourge of isolation, Jeanna reclaimed hope. As Grandma Dora stood rubbing her back soothingly, Jeanna, uttered, 'I'm so sorry Grandma for putting you through this, please forgive me'.

Grandma Dora eyes running, gazed lovingly at her second child and held Jeanna for what seemed an eternity, oblivious to the locked, impenetrable embrace between shared between Dot and Nathaniel. Their hold upon one another vanquished the heartache of decades past. 'I love you Dorothy Lynn Thornton, always have, always will'. As Nathaniel gently pecked Dotty's forehead, she held him closely, whispering, 'Always and forever, remember the promise we made?' Elated by his newfound bounty of joy, Nathaniel replied "Forever and One Day, beloved!' Jeanna squealed with joy, watching first loves ratify vows innocently spoken more than four decades ago.

Jeanna was overjoyed. It wasn't that euphoria-glazed confection of hope spoiled by the vicissitudes of living. No, this was a renewed faith in Love, in the audacious capacities of a Loving God who uses his creation in performing miracles every day within mundane human experience. Life, Jeanna realized, could be as extraordinary, or, as grindingly base as she wished. She discerned that every human battled conditions that were humbling and, at times crippling, Pastor Wade assured his flock one Sunday that His Grace was sufficient.

Dysthymia was her cross, a thorn in her frail flesh that no amount of human will alone could conquer. The condition could, however, be mastered, not just maintained. The latter required a defeatist disposition, the former, a determined outlook and sober acceptance mixed always with hope. This was no simple revelation; it was a transformative force in

Jeanna's soul. She knew with discipline, accountability and support, the effects of Dysthymia could be lessened over time, as each mountain, or mood was climbed with the support of family, friends and above all FAITH. Walking through valleys and shadows of death was never to be a lone sojourn. Jeanna would have to Trust God to be her Present Help and Strength. Jeanna slowly and with her grandmother's aid, stood, (Foley catheter and all), shakily at first, then she embraced two of the critical linchpins in her healing, who, like God, showed up in the nick of time. 'Mom', Jeanna spoke tentatively, 'Thank you for being here. I know you love me; I am so sorry for the invective-filled letter I sent you'.

Her joyful streams flowed uninhibited this time; for Dot, it had been decades since her only child uttered that coveted title, Mom. She was speechless, her heart full. Nathaniel, with mock jealousy asked, "Where is my hug, new-found daughter, and it better be a big one! It's been forty

-three years!' They held one another joyous tears flowing, as lost decades melted into moments, obliterating space and time, filling their losses with optimism that their best days lie ahead of them. 'Forever and a one day my dear daughter, always and forever you'll be Daddy's little girl.' Grandma Dora sat in the recliner, rejoicing solemnly remembering the promise of Romans 8:28, 'And we know that All things work together for the good of them that love God, to them who the called according to His Purpose'.

"Amen, Lord, praise sweet Jesus!" With that proclamation, she sat, watching her children hopefully. Exhaustedly she prepared for another 72-hour watch with Jeanna. She would see her through until the end. The most fitful sleepiness she had experienced in decades overtook her. Drowsily she mumbled, "Lord, It's on them now, my journey is over. They will see her through." The matriarch smirked while reviewing the 50 missed calls on her cell phone. "Oh well, the fallout has already begun from Jeanna's letters There is nothing I can do." With that thought, she turned off the phone, and smiled. "Maybe she should relocate... Let them deal with that too!" she chuckled. A final thought crossed her mind as she rested: 'Nathaniel, how are your parents doing?' Nathaniel smiled a knowing grin, and said, "Daddy is fine, Miss Dora."

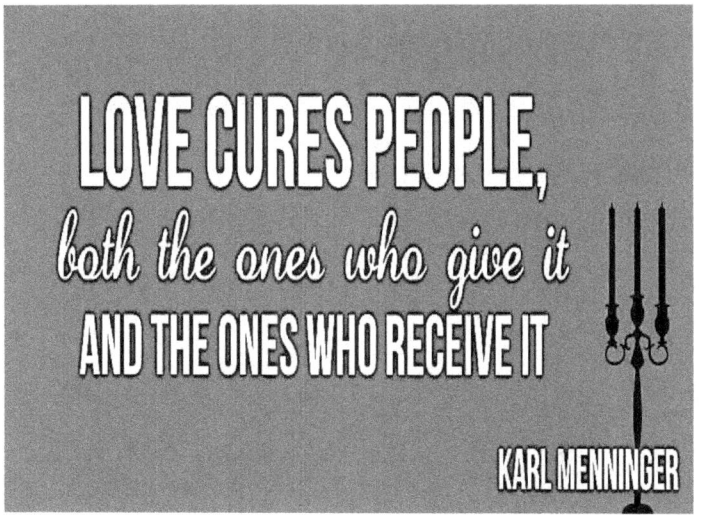

The End of Book 1

ABOUT THE AUTHOR

Roslyn J. Daniel began her writing career while studying English Literature and Social Work at Rutgers University. She enjoyed penning short stories, poetry and prose for weddings and other venues and developed an interest in suicidality after losing a cherished classmate to depression. Her works shed light on this phenomenon in positive and affirming light- the Love of God. Roslyn is also the founder of Artistic Overtures, a multifaceted event-planning and life coaching organization, under which she published this first in series of novels about Divine Intervention in the affairs of men. She is the proud mother of Rachel, who is preparing to enter Medical School in 2017. Look for more works on self-help and relationships in the Summer and Fall of 2016.

More Titles from Author Roslyn Daniel
(Coming Summer and Fall, 2016)

**A Series of Failed Suicidal Careers,
Book 2: Joel Brown**

Losers.com & Other Characters to Avoid Now

How to Get to Hell-Naw For Real

Why 21 Days to Change is Not Realistic

**How to Get Rid of the Enemy Between Your
Ears Without A Lobotomy**

Social Media Devotions and Prayers

The Real Cost of Your Low Self-Esteem

How to Set Yourself Free

How to Set Boundaries that Stick

Why You Don't Talk About Sex